SHINE ON,
MARQUEE MOON

SHINE ON, MARQUEE MOON

BY ZOË HOWE

Matador
9 Priory Business Park,
Wistow Road, Kibworth Beauchamp,
Leicestershire. LE8 0RX
Tel: 0116 279 2299
Email: books@troubador.co.uk
Web: www.troubador.co.uk/matador
Twitter: @matadorbooks

ISBN 978 1785893 162

British Library Cataloguing in Publication Data.
A catalogue record for this book is available from the British Library.

Printed and bound in the UK by TJ International, Padstow, Cornwall
Typeset in 11pt Garamond Pro by Troubador Publishing Ltd, Leicester, UK

Matador is an imprint of Troubador Publishing Ltd

MIX
Paper from
responsible sources
FSC® C013056

For Dylan

PROLOGUE

A new relationship – the prescient mingling of two record collections. A stark, sonic reflection of your partnership's potential, or lack of. Never mind compatibility tests and first-date small talk, whether or not someone is a suitable prospect can be divined by a glance across the spines of well-loved jewel cases and battered LPs. You are looking for the records that complement your collection, the records that suitably contrast, the records that, while they've been etched on your memory since childhood, you'd never got round to buying for yourself, and, most importantly, the records that double up with yours. There should always be a crossover. *Innervisions, Houses Of The Holy, Abbey Road, Horses.* Deal breakers all, for me at least. But the king of the deal breakers, the album I seek first, is Television's *Marquee Moon.* If it isn't there I'm not wasting my time.

Marquee Moon. Lower East Side punk at its most poetic, every luminous song evoking raw, familiar emotions. *Marquee Moon.* Too beautiful, sometimes, to listen to at all, depending on how you're feeling that day. Nick agreed. Nick had it on all formats. He had a framed poster of the album artwork on his wall, between the Hirsts and the Harings. I was always going to say yes to Nick.

It's 4pm and I'm driving west out of the city, brick-brown and grey turning green. This journey has nothing at the end of it, nothing specific – not for me. It is merely an opportunity to be alone for a few hours; a secret mission with no objective other than to briefly disappear. By moving at speed out of London through an indifferent landscape, I feel as if I'm leaving something behind, just for a while.

The sun is going down. Everything is pink. I turn my lights on, turn the radio on, turn the dial to the first station I find with any music. It's a pirate station, broadcasting presumably from someone's shed a few streets away. The DJ is playing obscure dub reggae but frequently turns the fader down mid-track to shout about a club night in Hanwell. I kind of like it. It's a distraction. And if I'm not distracting myself, I really am alone. Actually, it's worse than that; I don't mind being alone. But I'm alone with a sound in my head that doesn't go away no matter what music I pipe in. And no, it's not tinnitus, although I've got that too.

I have a voicemail message.

"Don't forget those trousers need fixing in time for the gig. That's important, Sylvie. They need double-stitching or… whatever. Just do what you have to do."

Les Tanner, manager of theatrical 80s pop band Concierge,

never says 'goodbye'; he just hangs up. In fact, he rarely says 'hello.' Just launches straight into his instructions which, today, concern stage clothes that have let their wearer down at the worst possible moment: whilst posturing in front of a crowd of fans. And, before you ask, that is my problem because I'm their dresser, and ripped crotches, loose buttons and the general pimping of designer garments are all very much my 'thing'. As it were. It's a gateway into something more creative, although the gate does seem to be a bit stiff at the moment.

Every communication from Les is a barked command, but something about his harassed, Estuarine voice anchors me. Without Les interrupting my train of thought, maybe I'd detach, float away. Maybe I'd find a hotel, stay a few nights, miss a few meetings, a few shows. Maybe I wouldn't come back. Les's messages keep the thread between me and my responsibilities pulled taut.

I'm tired now. I'd like to be in bed. I could have stayed in Nick's bed. Instead I randomly chose to drive out to a place called Garsby. It's very boring. Nick's bed isn't boring (I found a Roland Keytar in there the other night, the ridiculous keyboard/guitar hybrid beloved by 80s synth-pop stars the world over. He does play keyboards, but still, bit weird). Nick's bed is also so huge it wouldn't be out of place in *The Princess and the Pea*, if you subtracted the vegetables and popped a Keytar in there. But sometimes I need innocuous, anonymous space where there is, for once, no chance of being surprised, maddened, over-stimulated. Garsby's great for that.

One doesn't hit the road with a band and expect a peaceful, uncomplicated life. Sometimes I forget how much I miss a bit of calm. And then I realise I miss the chaos more, and go careering back to that. It's all about the contrast, and today I need calm and I need detachment – physical detachment – from London, from Nick. If I have that, just for a while, the widening psychological gulf might not seem so desperate. When I think about Nick, I feel as if I'm thinking about someone I'm still working out, rather than the man I fell in love with on tour. A 2-D figure; vague, out of focus and surrounded by a fair bit of dry ice.

Since we returned from Concierge's comeback tour (celebrated with only slight irony by the press), he's been distant, quieter. He was pretty monosyllabic in the first place. 'Adjusting', apparently. That I can relate to. We're all trying to navigate our way through this glittering otherworld of noise, dark corners and contradictions; a shinier, harder, dirtier side of life. If we only treated it like a glorified 'hop on/hop off' bus and took a chance to enjoy the view occasionally, some of us might even get off unscathed.

*

Last night was one thing. Last night was good. It started to go wrong when I came to this afternoon. September sunlight burning through the gap in the drapes, I lazily reached out an arm, only to be greeted by musky, sweat-damp sheets and a Post-it note, curling in the warmth of the room and sticking to the back of my hand.

'Back in a few hours. X'.

I propped myself up on one elbow, viewing the scene: empty tumblers on the floor, a boozy whiff still in the air; black tights merging with the overflowing contents of Nick's suitcase, a veritable oil-slick of over-priced clothes all in varying shades of black. (Nick lives out of his suitcase for at least a month after coming home; it helps him 'make the transition'. I believe it to be an excuse not to hang up his clothes or take them to the cleaners, but this is by the by.)

As I rubbed my forehead, a dull pain pulsing behind one eye, something pink fluttered onto my chest. Another bloody Post-it. He'd stuck it on my head when I was asleep. He hadn't written anything on this one, just stuck it there for his own amusement, and then left. It would have been cuter, I contemplated, had he then appeared from behind the door with some coffee. Maybe even an assortment of pastries. I sniffed for approaching croissants. Nothing.

These days Nick was either sleeping or absent, and the novelty of guessing where he was and what he was doing was wearing off, although it was clear this relatively new development would not be changing in any hurry. I'd have to get used to these little post-tour disappearances if any of this could continue to work. Perhaps I could. I knew this wasn't a 'normal' situation, I knew what not to expect. Let's face it; if you spent most of your life being pandered to, you'd find the concept of compromise somewhat alien yourself.

Basically, I loved him and I'd decided that, despite the sage advice given in a certain soft rock classic, sometimes love *is* enough, and that was just bloody well that. I'm aware ageing pop stars are fairly high up on the list of 'no-nos' when it comes to getting married in many people's eyes, but Nick, despite the implausibly black hair and penchant for sunglasses indoors, did manage to defy most clichés and was loyal and stoic, viewing the general circus with amusement and successfully maintaining a relative amount of dignity and was ageing gracefully, and, as far as the others were concerned, frustratingly slowly. He also had a gaze so hypnotic it could unravel secrets and expose liars with a single glower, depending on his level of sobriety. This may be why he tended to keep his eyes half-closed and under the blackest of Ray-Bans, as if conserving his ocular juju for when he really needed to vaporise someone. Alternatively he just needed more sleep. Either way, it worked for me.

Nick and I were powerfully attracted to each other from the moment we locked eyes; there was an energy that crackled between us to such an overwhelming extent I occasionally thought I might pass out. Everyone noticed it. You don't get much privacy on tour. He stole a kiss one night after summoning me to fix a button on his jacket that didn't actually need fixing. Things moved pretty rapidly after that. In fact, within three months we'd even decided to get engaged. I know. What happens on tour doesn't always stay on tour, but sometimes… well, maybe it should.

The proposal wasn't romantic in the conventional sense: I was loading the backstage washing-machine with sweat-stained stage towels when he just steamed in, grabbed me and muttered his intentions into my face with gin on his breath and the expression one might wear when telling someone there'd been a death in the family. "Marry me." More of a panicked demand than a question popped. Well, that's my Nick. I could tell it was sincere though, and sincerity counts for a lot, what with it being something of a rarity round these parts. The rest of the gang expressed their happiness for us in various ways:

"It's totally unprofessional," grumbled Les.

"Thanks, man."

"Nick has feelings! How about that?"

"Knew it was a matter of time – she was already doing his laundry every day after all!" guffawed Ron Gomez, Concierge's big-haired frontman. This became Gomez's catchphrase whenever the subject of our relationship came up. Once delivered, balance would simultaneously be restored by a stony glare from Nick, and about two seconds later Gomez would go off in a sulk.

This exchange was, if nothing else, one of life's little certainties. Another certainty was the acceptance that Gomez, like many in his position, was unable to take interest in any conversation that didn't focus on him. You don't have to ask how he is; he'll tell you anyway, in incredible detail. Don't expect a two-way conversation, mind. As soon as he stops expounding, he'll check his phone, tune his guitar or start whining about the rider. He might swagger to the bar to find someone sufficiently star-struck to listen to a barrage of boasting about things that mostly happened two decades ago. These are all things that might have irritated Nick more had he been inclined to have a conversation with him in the first place.

This should give you a good idea of how Gomez's mind works. I attended an after-show party shortly before my first night working with the band. Les, the manager, took my hand and led me up to Gomez to introduce me. Before Les could say any more than: "Ron, this is Sylvie…" Gomez shook his head sternly and said: "No, Les. Too young," before wandering off. It took me a few moments before I realised that Gomez had assumed I was a groupie, procured and then presented as some kind of post-show gift, a delicacy, like one of the canapés being handed around. "Too young." I guess it could have been worse.

Concierge was a curiously co-dependent operation, with thinly veiled hostilities simmering behind a slick front of professionalism. Despite what their fans wanted to think, they didn't hang out and 'jam' in their spare time, they weren't all living together in one house like The Monkees… they weren't that keen on each other at all. Considering the years they'd spent putting up with each other's idiosyncrasies, it was a wonder they'd still be up for working together, but, as the long-suffering Les would observe, everyone has their price, and Maseratis won't buy themselves.

For me, life on tour, with its twists, turns and revolving door of weirdos, was a bizarre kind of reality that I felt comfortable with. Put me in an office and I don't know what to do. Odd hours, big egos, Lurex – I could deal with those. What I was finding hard to manage was the fact that, while Nick and I had become almost inseparable on the road, I was only now getting used to being with my fiancé in a 'normal' setting back home in West London. Even though there was a wedding to plan and a diamond on the correct finger, life felt less stable, as if something had been shoved out of position.

When we were together, Nick treated me like a piece of crystal he was terrified of breaking, strangely reverent and devoted. We'd stay up all night and lie on the floor listening to the Cocteau Twins or Television by candle-light, drinking and smoking, talking and dreaming like we always did, but it felt different now. He was starting to withdraw.

Admittedly I'd been warned about this by the others. Touring wasn't for everyone but the hothouse nature of a travelling show suited Nick perfectly; it kept him in balance, propped him up, forcibly socialised him. He was so used to that vital support network, being at home was a culture shock that left him confused, even nervous. Time and space tend to go a little wonky on the road anyway, but it was as if Nick was trying to get used to a new time zone in a foreign land. I now had to make sure I didn't see him too often in case his behaviour knocked my own balance out of whack. I wanted to help, but that wasn't easy when he was becoming so evasive. If this was the way he was, I told myself, I'd learn to work around it. Sometimes I'd wonder whether he'd do the same for me if the roles were reversed. Maybe.

The explanation would usually be that he needed 'space' and so would either be in his car, driving aimlessly around Richmond and Twickenham, or seeking out his favourite brand of cigarettes: Sobranie Black Russians; hard to find but worth it. Black with gold tips… they coordinated perfectly with his hair and wardrobe, which is obviously important. Alternatively he could be walking Brando, his elderly Basset Hound, or reading under a tree in the Old Deer Park, close to his magnificent Gothic home nearby. Yes, pop sure could pay, and Nick Sinclair was, to be fair, a star of a certain vintage. Richmond, with its Rolling Stones, riverboats and agreeable blend of beatnik vibes and easy wealth, attracted him, and he bought a house there as soon as his first record advance came through in 1983. Fortunately for him, Concierge were at their prime when record labels still had money to throw at bands, and no one had started downloading anything for free yet. In fact, no one had started downloading anything at all.

By now, my dreamy state had dissolved. We'd planned to spend what was left of the day together. Nick will have meant it when he suggested it, but that was last night, and he was a present tense kind of a guy. He'd have married me in the nearest registry office the day he'd proposed if we hadn't been in an unlovely part of Solihull at the time. I'm not one of those girls who starts planning their wedding at the age of five, but be fair.

Wrapping myself in a sheet, I looked out of the window to see Nick's black Citroën in the forecourt. I called his name. Nothing.

Walking Brando then. I twisted my hair into a tangled bun and padded to the bathroom, treading on soft, expensive clothes as I went.

The sound of water rushing into the bath pierced the silence of the house, and as the tub slowly filled I opened a window to admire the garden; wild and a little gloomy, a ceiling of tree-tops knitting their branches together as if protecting some invisible secret that lay below. I loved this garden: the silver birches swaying at the bottom, the roses clinging heavily to the trellis, occasional cameos from next door's tabby, who was currently staring single-mindedly into the fish-pond at Nick's koi carp, bottom waggling in preparation for a move he would undoubtedly regret. I could also see the chunky shape of Brando, happily oblivious to the fact there was a cat nearby. So… cigarettes and a drift to the Old Deer Park, I guessed. Brando had evidently braved the dog-flap and taken himself for his own walk. A draught rushed in, causing the window to clatter shut.

The bath water was stone cold. Cursing quietly, I pushed my feet into Nick's too-big slippers and carefully shuffled downstairs to check the boiler.

As I descended, I touched the framed *Marquee Moon* cover as I always did, OCD, fingertips in the dust drawing imaginary strength from Tom Verlaine. I'd gaze upon him the way some would meditate over an icon of the Virgin Mary or a pendant embossed with the image of St Christopher. *Marquee Moon* was my protective talisman and boy, did I feel like I needed one in here.

This house was not my friend. I didn't feel welcome. It was awe-inspiring but there was nothing happy about it. When Nick was here it wasn't so bad, but whenever I was alone – which I increasingly was – the energy of the place seemed to sag. It felt wrong, as if something dark was dripping from the ceilings and clinging to the walls. Nick had, rather sweetly, set up a room for me with a table and a record player where I could paint and make collages and sketch out ideas – in theory it was perfect, freshly decorated, overlooking the garden – but I didn't even really feel welcome in there.

The stairs creaked in response to my footsteps, and I glanced at the paintings and prints that dotted the walls as I went: everything from Matisse to Hockney to Keith Haring, all jostling for attention. I didn't want to know how much Nick had spent on art over the years, although it was more sensible than spending all of his spare cash on cars he would never drive, stupidly expensive meals he would never remember or extravagant holidays he would probably just sleep through. He'd recently acquired one of Damien Hirst's midnight-blue skull paintings, which I refused to look at, especially if I had to go downstairs in the night for a glass of water. The sight of a grinning skull gleaming in the moonlight in such an old, weird house could be too much. I was already paranoid that some psychotic Mrs Danvers-type creature was going to appear from the shadows when I least expected it.

Yes, Nick had been cleverer with his money than the others in the band, but he also had better taste than say, Gomez with his nouveau riche Essex pad, or Johnson Large, the drummer, whose pseudonym sort of says it all when it comes to taste. Johnson, incidentally, had been in a squat rock group called Arse? (the question mark was his idea) before joining Concierge – but he'd since decided that living in a house with a pool and a private cinema suited him better. The days of communal living with his Arse? comrades were now comfortingly far away. And then there was Abra, the dynamic replacement for the original bass-player – a chain-smoking lunatic known as Henson Bedges (real name Malcolm Bunt. Allegedly set fire to himself in 1996). I still have no idea what Abra's house is like; she spends most of her time sofa-surfing when not on tour, but if her home is anything like her wardrobe, then I'm thinking *Foxy Brown* via *Star Trek*.

It was the record label's decision to bring her in, and it was a smart move, although the rest of Concierge were a little apprehensive at first. Feminism had passed most of them by during the 80s and 90s, but Abra put paid to that. Abra's just amazing. You couldn't blame this old-fashioned bunch for being uncertain at first, but shock's good for people. Unless it gives you a heart attack, of course. Or kills you. Other than that, I'm all for some good old shocking to prevent people like Concierge getting set in their ways.

Stepping into the chilly, stone-floored kitchen, I was jolted out of my thoughts, the characters in my head vanishing instantly. I was sure I'd heard what could only be described as a quiet exhalation of breath, followed by an insistent tapping and a flurry of indistinct sounds. The house was so quiet, any noise jumped out at you. I always got spooked – it was hard not to at Nick's place – but it was generally just something outside, or a radiator cooling down, or just the house settling. This time I knew it was different. I experienced a sharp stab of a bad, bad feeling. I looked through the kitchen window into the back garden. Brando was still mooching in the distance. Great guard-dog. I eased my feet out of Nick's slippers and stepped back into the musty hall to face the drawing room. When Nick first gave me the tour of the house, he'd guided me past this room, simply explaining it was locked, unused, he'd lost the key years ago. The sounds were coming from behind this door.

I called his name again and listened hard, frustrated by another few seconds of silence. My mind raced, but as I tried to rationalise what I'd just heard, I felt as if every cell in my body had frozen again. Two more little taps, and then a muffled sigh, soft but unmistakable.

As soon as I could convince my body to move, I was upstairs, pushing myself haphazardly into clothes, ramming feet into tights and shoes, running back down the stairs and out, the locks and chains of the front door still clattering and swinging as I reversed out of the drive. You know the rest. Nick was expecting me that night. Nick could whistle.

My terraced house in Strawberry Hill seemed to glow in the fading light as I approached. Nothing felt like coming home, especially today. The drive had separated me from the noises, the feelings, the fear – it had helped me at least approach some sense of perspective. Now I was back, and so was the anxiety. So, too, was that sigh, echoing horribly in my head, unearthly, not quite male, not quite female, but human. I turned up the radio in an attempt to drown it out. Collapsing onto the sofa with my bags around me, I felt for my phone. Time to text Nick. My version of his Post-it.

'Something came up. See you in the week. Sylv X'

That was all I could bring myself to say. I didn't mind him knowing I was irked by another let-down of a day courtesy of his increasingly tiresome disappearing act, but if I was going to make any reference to what I'd heard, it couldn't be in a text. He probably wouldn't take it seriously, and I was in no mood to be laughed at. I lay back and stared at the portrait of Patti Smith on the facing wall; white shirt, black tie, strength and wisdom and a touch of mischief shining from her dark eyes and radiating from her slight frame. She'd know what to do. She'd seen it all before.

I knew who would take my story seriously. Very seriously. Possibly too seriously, but I had to talk to someone, and I was tempted to make that someone Betty Sinclair – wise woman extraordinaire, spiritually attuned earth goddess and, perhaps most importantly, Nick's older sister.

Whilst on tour, I'd become absorbed whether I liked it or not – mostly I liked it – into what was known affectionately as 'the Coven'; a kind of rock 'n' roll Women's Institute, if you will. The Coven was presided over by Betty, who had assimilated herself into the crew during the 1980s when Concierge's wardrobe department needed extra assistance. Betty still travelled with the band, helping me when I joined the crew and generally being a welcome matriarchal presence on an otherwise very male touring show. She was Mother Superior of the road, a terrible but determined cook and a walking New Age emporium, weighed down by gemstones and amulets and endlessly wishing people 'Love and Light', which garnered a mixed response, particularly from the roadies.

This excitable, highly perfumed collective (the Coven, as opposed to the roadies – although they could be quite fragrant at times themselves) was occasionally enhanced by the presence of Abra, and was completed by Gomez's wife and also his lover, both of whom seemed happy sharing their duties of fussing over Gomez when his mullet required primping, his lunchtime aperitif preparing or simply when he was behaving like a big baby, which was most of the time. The entire operation was bemusing, but… well, whatever works. Nick always insisted that Gomez was suffering from an affliction which meant he needed constant attention. "It's known as lead-singeritis," he'd tell me gravely. Huffs, tantrums and flouncing were daily occurrences, and naturally the roar of the crowd was one of the few remedies that could ease his pain. Once onstage, conflicts were forgotten, sour exchanges neutralised and bruised egos would suddenly heal. Or at least his would.

Pearl, Gomez's wife, was an ageing Essex girl with streaked blonde hair and a passion for baking and fetish. Pearl, when not fluttering around Gomez, would spend her time making dubious-looking cakes, polishing her rubber-wear and hanging out with Ange, a weathered glamour puss with a Bisto tan, an abrasively cheerful personality and a tremendous capacity for cocaine. Together they were quite a team.

The Coven, the band and the crew really were like family to me, like a crazed bunch of aunts and uncles, and I adored them. I definitely spent more time with them than anyone I was related to. I was an only child and my parents had left England for Majorca years ago, gradually changing in hue from what the fashion industry calls 'greige' to somewhere between Fanta and freshly oiled teak.

I missed the Concierge clan once we'd returned home: life suddenly moved at an entirely different pace, and while the Coven tried to meet every couple of weeks, it wasn't the same as practically living with each other. One of the things I loved about them was how easy it was to tell them anything; nothing was too outrageous, and there was something about the transient lifestyle that made you feel safe, as if you shed a skin every time you left for the next city. Staying in one place felt stagnant, but moving on felt healthy. How healthy we actually were was up for debate.

Anyway. Betty. As Nick's sister, she was a little close for comfort, but I could rely on her, and besides, what I needed to talk about did sound like her territory. But would even Betty find it unbelievable? Would she think I was mad? Rationally speaking, this was unlikely. I could dress a ferret as Madonna and train it to play the banjo and only then would I be approaching the levels of insanity that the others had already sailed past, waving merrily as they went.

After making a pot of tea (sugar stirred in for the shock) and digging out the duty-free Daim bars from the cupboard (again, for the shock), I called Betty's landline. She only lived in Barnes; I could be there in minutes.

"Haaaaallo?"

"Betty, it's… "

"Gotcha! Leave a message and I'll call you back. Love and light!"

Christ. I tried her mobile.

"Haaaaallo?"

I wasn't falling for it this time.

"Hello?"

Extremely amusing…

"Is that you, Sylvie?"

"Oh! I thought it had gone to voicemail."

"Really?" Betty didn't seem to have the remotest concept of what I was on about.

"Anyway, I was wondering whether we could have a chat, I'm a bit worried about something."

"Wedding jitters?" There was a smile in her voice. She was ready to play big sister and allay matrimonial fears I hadn't even considered yet.

"We're not even close to making a plan, you know that."

"Ah," Betty said knowingly. "How long has it been?"

"Sorry?"

"Since your period?"

"It's nothing like that! It's complicated. I just wanted to— "

"We should have a Coven Meeting," decided Betty.

"Well, really I was just thinking— "

"COVEN MEETING. Come on, we must be due one. Why don't we just have the meeting now? I've got the Essex contingent here playing gin rummy. I'll ring Abra, and… "

"Don't. I'll see how I feel. Thanks."

"Whatevs. L and L!" And she was gone.

I exhaled, realising I'd been holding my breath, and dipped a Daim bar into the hot tea, stirring it around and nibbling at the melted bits, free hand scrabbling for the remote. There was nothing on TV but I didn't care. With the low chunnering of Radio 4 mingling oddly with a *Cheers!* re-run, I fell into a doze, sweet wrappers in my lap and tea cooling by my side.

Tap-tap. I furrowed my brow in my half-sleep. *Tap-tap-tap.* Only this time it was louder, more insistent. There was something different about the tone. I opened my eyes, as if expecting to catch sight of something before it dematerialised. Nothing. I brushed the wrappers and chocolate shards off my lap with an irascible swipe. Now I wasn't just spooked, I was fed-up. The sounds I'd heard had wormed their way into my sub-conscious and now I couldn't even drift into a nap in peace.

TAP-TAP-TAP. The door. It was just the front door. It sounded like someone tapping their nails against the glass panel at the top. Whoever it was, they were very insistent; normally whoever was knocking would bugger off after the first couple of attempts. I wasn't a big fan of answering the door. It was generally someone trying to sell me something or someone trying to convert me to something, or maybe a nosy neighbour hoping to catch sight of Nick. If it was someone I knew, they'd call me first. But this visitor wasn't going anywhere.

Through the frosted glass at the top of the door I observed the blurred forms of a large Rula Lenska-red hairdo, flanked by, on one side, a blonde head with a purple streak, and on the other, a platinum Afro. Either this was an alternative carolling troupe getting their practise in early or…

"Sylvie? Let us in!"

… or the Coven were here, love-bomb ready to detonate. In they trooped, led by their commanding officer Betty, a symphony in red and purple chiffon. She was followed by Abra, Pearl and Ange, all of them planting waxy lipstick kisses on my cheeks before excitedly pushing past me into the house. Within seconds they were taking over the kitchen, unpacking goodies from expensive mini-markets before charging into the living room and plumping down severally on the sofa. Pearl slapped an already open packet of chocolate biscuits onto the coffee table (I observed a telltale line of crumbs on her neckline). This was the first time I'd seen the Coven en masse since the tour. It was startling.

"Well," I breathed once the women had settled down, a riot of big hair and clashing perfumes. "Tea?"

The cacophony started again as they all bounded back to their feet, crashing their way into the kitchen as if it were a race, insisting on making it themselves. Abra pinned me into my seat, arranging a cushion behind my head with grim concentration. "You've got to rest," she commanded. "We'll take care of all that." If this was an attempt at intimidating me into submission, it was effective. I obeyed, not that I had a choice, but right now I was more concerned about what the hell Betty had told the others.

Once the clatter of crockery had subsided and a grand display of teacups, biscuits, cake and novelty Elvis teapot had been arranged on the table, everyone turned to look at me with twinkling anticipation. I stared back, waiting for someone to speak. This was going to be interesting.

"It might not be, you know," ventured Pearl between dainty nibbles of biscuit, latex squeaking as she leaned forward. She gave a little wince.

"Might not be what?"

"You know. The missed period. Could be stress."

"I haven't missed a period!"

Everyone's eyes shot over to Betty, who now seemed extremely interested in the pattern on the arm of the chair. "I thought you just didn't want to talk about it over the phone," she muttered, pulling at a loose thread like a sulky teenager.

"PMT," announced Ange, trying to muster up a sympathetic facial expression. The Botox didn't allow for this. It's the thought that counts.

"It's literally nothing to do with my womb!" I heard myself snapping more loudly than I'd intended. It had the desired effect though; they were silent for once. I hadn't really reckoned on trying to explain what I'd heard – what I thought I'd heard – to all of them in one go.

Betty leant forward with a confidential air. "Is it the full moon?" Abra released a sigh of exasperation, which caused me to start. "It's a full moon in Scorpio on the weekend," continued Betty. "A lot of tension flying around. I read about it on Shelley Von Strunckel's website."

"Shelley Von… "

"Strunckel," Betty said sharply. "Not to mention the self-discovery it tends to prompt." I had to nip this firmly in the bud. It helped that Betty was of an esoteric bent, but only if she allowed me to get a word in.

"No, Betty. I don't think it's the full moon."

"Is it Nick?" offered Abra through mouthfuls of biscuit. "The idea of being tied to him for all eternity? I mean, he is quite dull."

"He's deep!"

"Deeply dull."

"There's a lot to be said for a bit of depth. Anyway, he's not dull, he's enigmatic," I insisted. "And he looks a bit like Tom Hiddleston in *The Avengers*… if the light's right."

"Yes!" said Pearl. "He's totally Loki. I'll never be able to watch *Thor* again without thinking of Nick."

"Loki would be easier to hang out with," added Ange, tossing her Tina Turner locks. "Nick's no fun. Nick's the anti-fun. I mean, he barely speaks."

"To you," I said.

"He can be pretty morose," admitted Betty between sips of sugary tea. "'Silent Silas' our mum used to call him." Chuckling as the memories trickled forth, she hoisted herself out of her seat and trotted to the loo. It was just as well Betty had left the room on that note, as no one wanted to hear *that* story again. But you're about to.

Betty took after her flamboyant mother Marina, a self-styled libertine who eventually left the country with a Moroccan lover in 1981. Nick, on the other hand, went to great pains not to take after anyone in his family at all.

The dominant Marina held her husband Ted Sinclair in fairly low regard. There was nothing essentially wrong with Ted; he was a gentle soul, but the pair grew apart when, during the late 1960s, the Sinclairs moved from North London to the witchy New Forest. Ted took a job as a bank clerk in the market town of Ringwood while Marina – and Betty – were soaking up the atmosphere of their new habitat.

Marina was becoming less interested in conventional family life and, encouraged by her progressive New Forest neighbours, was now more interested in aromatherapy, which led to crystal healing, which led to massage, which, somehow, led to nude yoga sessions in forest glades and eventually led to tantric sex, not necessarily with her husband.

The unfortunate Ted went into a nervous decline, taking a turn for the worse when Marina announced she wanted a threesome with two men, neither of whom were him. A year later he suffered a fatal heart attack, Betty joined a commune and Marina was left, for the time being, with Silent Silas. Poor Nick. It explained so much.

"So? What the bloody hell is it?" said Ange, after releasing a thunderous belch. She was foregoing the tea, sipping straight from a hip-flask which had evidently been in constant use throughout the day.

"OK! This is going to sound weird, so bear with me. And don't laugh. And… Betty, I love you, but I really need you to not interrupt."

"You've set a date for the big day!" interrupted Betty.

"What did I just say?"

"Let her speak, Betty," said Abra, throwing the scrunched-up biscuit packet in her direction. "This sounds serious."

*

"Wow. Can *you* get me some acid then, Sylv?"

Yes. As I'd feared, telling this lot that I basically thought Nick's house was playing host to a spectral presence prompted considerable derision. To be fair, most of them hadn't even been inside it.

One person wasn't laughing. "Sylvie," said Betty, flapping her hands at the others to shut them up and sending an exotic whiff of Shalimar into the air. "You were right to mention this. I've always felt Nick's house had an unsettled atmosphere. Let's not beat around the bush, the place is totally haunted," she said, thoroughly enjoying herself.

"Now this tapping, this sigh… " An image flickered briefly in Betty's mind, and she gave a little shudder, as if she was shaking something off. I waited patiently for The Oracle to calm down while the rest of the Coven mumbled between themselves.

"Ladies," Betty announced. "There's only one thing for it."

"Not a séance," groaned Ange.

"A séance," concluded Betty. She finally had a legitimate chance for one and she wasn't going to waste it. I looked at that earnest face. Hell, it wasn't like I had any better ideas. I started clearing away glasses, cups and biscuit packets.

"What are you doing?" said Betty with the sort of incredulity that would only be justified if I was, say, taking off all of my clothes or rubbing jam into my hair.

"Preparing for the séance? We need to sit and do the… hand thing? On the table?" I didn't understand what she didn't understand. This was her idea.

"No, no, no," said Betty. "We're not doing it here. We have to do it at Nick's place. At the source."

The source. I felt a chill at the thought of even going back to 'the source', let alone trying to contact whatever was there, tapping things and, well, exhaling all over the place. I was there again in my mind, outside that door, moments from hearing the sigh…

"We'll go over on Saturday night, the band have a rehearsal for that charity show, so Nick will be out of the way. And it's a full moon— "

"In Scorpio!" chorused Ange and Pearl.

"So it's the ideal time for otherworldly practices. Tapping, knocking, these things are all signs that something is trying to get a message through. Maybe we should make it a bit easier for this lost soul, and shoo it towards the light."

"There's only one lost soul in Nick's house," sniggered Ange.

"OK," I said, ignoring her. "Let's do it."

So we had a plan. I didn't like it much, but it was a plan, and I was no longer alone with that all too recent memory. After everyone had finally gone, I went straight to bed, ignoring the post-Coven debris in the living room. I could deal with it tomorrow.

My bedroom felt like a fridge after two nights at Nick's, so I tweaked the radiator and quickly changed into my warmest pyjamas. I resolved to keep a lamp on and have the radio playing quietly; too dark and my imagination would run wild, too quiet and the sounds would creep back into my mind. I put my phone on charge amid the unread books and tangled jewellery on my bedside table and lay back onto the cold pillow.

It had been good to fill my house with warmth and chatter, but I couldn't shake the feeling that I was deceiving Nick, sharing my fears with the Coven and not him, and then planning what felt like an elaborate supernatural mission in his own house for when he was safely out of the way. But I was curious too.

The charging mobile beeped as it came back to life, giving my nerves another start. It was Nick. 'Got your text. What happened to today?' Bit rich. His text had been sent at 9pm, a good six hours after I'd scarpered. These lapses were hard to get used to. I didn't know whether I wanted to get used to them anymore. But we'd come this far. We loved each other. It was up to me to find out what was pushing him into these bouts of solitude. His band-mates were needy and high-maintenance; by contrast Nick seemed together, self-contained. Perhaps we had all overestimated him. Whatever the answer was, this required careful handling, and I wasn't sure yet what that entailed.

Usually I prided myself on knowing exactly what to do. I was always the one who was positive, strong, in control. Right now I didn't feel any of these things. I stared at the pale shimmer of the moon, shining through the thin blind. Full moon on Saturday. Like I could forget.

Too wound-up to sleep, I scrolled through pictures on my mobile until my eyes grew tired, pausing on a picture of Nick and me at the seaside. Blackpool, off-season. I stared at the image, taking in every detail; the steel-grey Northern sky merging with the churning brine, the seagull eyeing our chips, the incline of Nick's head, the dot of red lipstick on my teeth. That picture encapsulated everything we felt on that long tour: happy and in love and secure inside that protective microcosm, almost communicating by telepathy by the end of it. Nick was right. Life was so much simpler on the road, everyone knew the roles they had to play. Now we were rudderless, floundering. It was time to improvise, and some of us were better at that than others.

"Nick!" Betty's voice ripped into the morning air as she rang the doorbell repeatedly, sending ravens flapping out of trees and prompting a desultory bark from Brando. Shuffling feet eventually approached and the long process of chains being unchained and locks being unlocked began. And then he appeared, like a rock 'n' roll Cousin It, squinting in the unfamiliar daylight.

"Good morning," said Betty, breezing past the apparition into the kitchen while Nick re-chained the door. Betty clicked on the kettle and, as her brother sloped into the room, eyes half-shut and head lolling to one side like an off-duty marionette, she peered at him. "Where the hell did that awful kimono come from?"

"What? The... this? You gave it to me," he managed, pulling the offending robe around himself. Verbally he was doing well considering he didn't normally speak at all before 1pm.

"You've probably done it up wrong. God, you're pale. And look at your eyes!"

"I can't look at my eyes. They're my eyes."

"Oh, you're in one of those moods." Betty found two faded black Concierge mugs (bearing the words 'THE Farewell Tour 1994!' in a shouty font – they'd had two farewell tours already by that point) and started making coffee with unnecessary flourish. As the water was poured, Betty held out her free hand gracefully to the side, like a high-wire artist keeping balance. Sugar lumps were dropped from a height, and the stirring of the coffee was a ceremony in itself, concluding with a rhythmic thwacking of spoon against cup to shake off the droplets. Nick knew it was coming and still winced against the high frequency racket of metal meeting china.

"So… " he ventured.

"Why am I here? I didn't know there was a law against visiting my own brother." Nick silently took the coffee that had been shoved in his direction and glanced up at the kitchen clock. 11.30am. Bloody hell.

Betty suddenly looked far away, as if she was trying to listen for something. She wanted to hear those noises for herself. Her bejewelled fingers felt for the radio by the kettle and turned down the volume.

"Oi, I was listening to that. Kind of."

"Classical music? Really?"

Nick shrugged. He had, as of last night, started leaving the radio on, tuned to Radio 3. It 'neutralised his ears', as he put it, and eased him in and out of the day, or that was the theory. This particular concerto featured more jabbing violins than *Psycho* and was easing him into hypertension more than anything else. Last night he tried to wind down to the relentless clanging of The Anvil Chorus.

"Anyway, what's the matter? What did you think you'd heard?"

"Oh, nothing! Nothing. Probably just the dog." She was struggling. Fortunately Nick didn't seem to notice or care.

"Bet, have you spoken to Sylvie?"

"Yes! Yes I have," she said, happy that the subject had changed.

"Well?"

"What?"

"Sylvie?"

"Ah yes. I saw her last night," said Betty absently, trying to case out the vibrations. She couldn't feel anything, but if anyone was determined to discover that there was something paranormal going on, it was her. Anything would be better than… well, than the alternative. She couldn't allow herself to believe it was that. Ghosts were easier to deal with than humans, in her opinion. This human, at least.

"And?" persisted Nick. "Is she all right? Yesterday she was here and then she just disappeared."

"One of your specialities, indeed."

Nick shifted. "That's me. It's not like *her*."

Betty looked at him evenly. "I'm just going to say this so we can get it out of the way. I know you find it hard being back, yadda yadda, but you've gone particularly odd this time, if you don't mind me saying." She watched his face for flickers of guilt. Nothing, it was just blank, waiting for her to get to the point. "You're not… "

"Not what?"

"You know. *You* know. Fuck it, Nick, you'd better not be." He continued to look at her without expression. "For Christ's sake, I'm talking about smack."

Nick closed his eyes. "What do you think?"

What did she think? She thought it wasn't out of the question. She was getting déjà vu. The way he looked, the way he acted, the disappearances. Textbook Junkie Behaviour. The problem was that Textbook Junkie Behaviour was just a slight magnification of Textbook Nick Behaviour.

"That's not an answer."

"No, Betty. No. There's your answer. Now you can answer my question. Sylvie," he repeated. "She hasn't responded to my text from last night. I guess she could be asleep; it's still kind of early," he added, pointedly. Betty wasn't rising to that, she got up every day at 7am to meditate, and besides, she was now focusing on the matter in hand: 1) Making sure Nick was definitely out on Saturday night, and 2) Making sure she could get into the house to prepare and have a snoop around. She'd been genuinely longing to have a séance in there for ages anyway, it was perfect – but she'd also have an opportunity to surreptitiously case the joint for drug paraphernalia.

"It's a strange old house, this? Isn't it?" she said incongruously, after a pause. "So much history, the walls must be hanging on to some memories."

"Hm." Nick had switched on his mental screen-saver and was now gazing out of the window at a cobweb. He found Betty's superstitions irritating and had constructed an automatic radar for when she was going to start prescribing crystals for his melancholia or flower remedies for his prostate or…

"Do you ever feel as if you're not entirely alone here?" she ventured, twisting her enormous topaz ring around her finger. "Do you ever feel a bit, I don't know… funny here?" She looked at him. He stared back inscrutably. There's nothing funny about him, she thought. Nothing funny 'ha-ha', anyway. "Well, I know I do," persisted Betty. Nick simply lit a cigarette and sat up at the breakfast bar. Having successfully frozen out an unnecessary metaphysical conversation, he looked at her, wondering what else was coming.

"So, Saturday night," Betty began. "You're rehearsing in town?"

"Rehearsing yes, in town no."

"Not here?" said Betty, a little too anxiously. Nick did sometimes use the basement as a rehearsal studio. It would scupper her entire plan, and she hadn't even made a plan yet.

"No, the damp makes Gomez's hair go frizzy. We'll be at Johnson's studio in Tring."

Perfect. Sessions at Johnson's studio generally went on until dawn mainly because Johnson, enjoying the rare opportunity to be in charge, took so long fiddling with knobs and repositioning microphone stands that it was midnight before anything got done. Add to that the fact most of them would be completely stoned by the time the studio was deemed ready and you had an all-nighter on your hands. Betty took a sip of coffee and tried to be casual.

"Need someone to look after Bongo?" she asked.

"Brando," corrected Nick, aware she was doing it on purpose. "Actually that would be great." He was slightly fazed by this. Betty had little time for the mutt. It would normally be easier to tell Betty to go out without make-up than ask her to look after 'Bongo'. "I was going to ask Sam to drop in and check on his Chudleys but…"

"His… Chudleys?" Betty wasn't sure whether this was some kind of code but she was fairly certain she didn't want to be going near any Chudleys.

"Special organic dog food with vitamins," he sighed. "I'll put some out but it might need topping up. He'll also need an evening walk. Garden will do. And you two can bond at last." His thin, bluish lips curved slightly into a smile.

"And what about your vitamins, Edward Scissorhands? You're not looking good, you know."

"Thanks."

"And who, pray tell, is 'Sam'?" enquired Betty.

"New roadie," said Nick, flicking through the copy of *Synth Quarterly* on the worktop. It had a picture of him on the cover, dead-eyed and pouting. "You'll meet him if you stick around, he's coming to sort out some gear for me in a bit."

Betty blanched. "No… "

"What? Not that kind of gear! GOD! Equipment kind of gear. E-quip-ment." Nick took a sharp drag from his cigarette and continued reading the same sentence over and over again, eyes ablaze.

This was a subject that had not been touched on, not really, for more than a decade. It had stayed safely in the dark, inert, not dead but sleeping, a no-go subject within the circle. It was certainly never discussed with anyone new. The secret had been kept from Abra and, most fastidiously, from me.

Just after Concierge first announced they were going to split,

Nick had slumped into a depression. He felt he was losing his purpose and his dysfunctional quasi-family all at the same time. Coke and champagne had been ever-present while Concierge were at their peak. "No snow? No show," Gomez would proclaim. "No Chandon, no band on." Words to live by, I'm sure you'll all agree. Weed and beer were part of the fabric of everyday life. But, despite the constant attentions of dealers during their glory years, they had all managed to avoid heroin. All except one. Lonely and listless after the break-up, Nick finally said yes. It wrapped him up, filled the void. He spent the years that followed chasing a high he'd never reach again.

Nick's band-mates were aware of this, but as they started living their lives increasingly separately, it was Betty who bore the brunt of the situation. With his sister at his side, Nick spent a great deal of time and money at a secluded rehab clinic in the late 1990s, and, once clean, he eventually started working again. But he was never the same, and neither was Betty. The emotional scars remained, although she'd dulled the pain in therapy. Part of the reason she was such a constant on tour was because she wanted to keep a close eye on her brother. If some parasite came along at the right moment, it wouldn't take much before he'd be back in the grip of it again. But nobody talked about it. It was best not to go there. It wasn't just the drug; it was the associations, the people and the places it had taken Nick to, the person it made him become, temporarily. This was a new era: the band was back together, he was relatively healthy and he'd found someone who loved him for the right reasons, and accepted that sometimes he needed space. Lots of it.

Betty had started reading the back of the Chudleys packet to curry favour and pass the time during the awful silence when there was a knock at the door. Nick slid off his stool and wandered with no great urgency into the hall to begin the interminable unlocking process. At least this would break the tension. Betty opened the kitchen window and leaned out to see Sam, presumably, waiting to be let in. "He'll only be another forty-five minutes!" she called, taking in his slightly bemused expression before ducking back inside.

Sam Lowther was in his late thirties – nothing wrong with the younger man; far from it, in Betty's eyes – and he was handsome, leonine, with thick, blondish hair and what Betty called 'a nice face'. He certainly made a change from the usual roadies in the Concierge crew, a hairy coming-together of unusual odours, moth-eaten band T-shirts, distended girths and combat shorts displaying kneecaps no one wanted to see.

"Cup of tea, Sam?" she called in a contrived sing-song voice, filling the kettle again and hunting for biscuits. It was all very well for Brando and his Chudleys; where were the treats for humans in this place? She located some Rich Teas – Nick had simple tastes in the biscuit department – and fanned them out on a plate.

"Thanks, don't mind if I do," came the response. A Northerner, eh? Betty liked Northerners. Nick trudged back into the kitchen, reluctantly ushering in Sam. "This is Betty, my older sister."

"Not that much older," said Betty quickly, sailing up to Sam, shawl undulating. He grinned and stuck out a hand in greeting. "Oh, I think we can do better than that!" she teased, opening her arms for a hug. Nick rolled his eyes as he loped off to sort out his keyboards, leaving Sam-Lowther-The-Northerner-With-The-Nice-Face to fend for himself.

Sam awkwardly accepted an embrace. "Ooh," smarmed Betty, "I knew you'd smell nice. What is it?"

"Erm… "

"Just you, I expect." Her eyes gleamed as she pushed a cup of tea towards him. "I didn't put sugar in. Sweet enough, I'd imagine."

Sam squirmed under her gaze, took the tea and started backing away slowly. "Better get back to Nick," he laughed nervously. Betty winked as he continued reversing into the hall.

"Stop it!" hissed Nick through the kitchen door, jerking her out of a swiftly-forming fantasy.

"I can't stop 'it', darling. I've got 'it'. Nothing I can do about that." She raised one shoulder coquettishly to her cheek. Maybe it was unfair, but few things made Nick want to puke more than seeing his fifty-five-year-old sister prowling around men who were young enough to be her sons – even if he was also surrounded by middle-aged men who routinely got busy with nubile women, or at least tried to. For some reason, in his eyes, there was just no comparison, not least because it reminded him too much of their gadabout mother.

He couldn't take it any more. He marched towards her, taking her cup from her hand. "Maybe you should start making tracks, Sis," he said, guiding her through the open front door and towards the racing green MG in the drive. "Here's a set of keys for Saturday, and remember he'll need a walk— "

"All right, all right," huffed Betty, craning sneakily for a last glimpse of Sam's denim-clad derrière as he lifted an amplifier into the van. "Bye, Sam!"

"Unbelievable," said Nick quietly, shutting her car door firmly as she waved through the window. Betty couldn't wait to tell the rest of the Coven about this.

"PARDON?"

"I said, I can't hear you properly, it's the delay," I said, trying to keep a grip on my patience.

"EH?"

"I said, I can't hear you, Dad. Shouting isn't helping."

"IT'S NO GOOD, SYLV. WE CAN'T HEAR YOU. IT'S THIS FLIPPING DELAY."

I refused to allow my face to show any irritation; they could see me after all, and the camera had a habit of freezing on the worst possible expressions. "I'll look at my settings," I sighed, shutting my laptop and lighting a cigarette. It was midday on Friday, and, for me, that meant a catch-up with the folks. They were Skype evangelists and as a result took a dim view of anyone who used anything as archaic as a phone to make an international call.

Every week Mum and Dad put on white linen clothes to show off their brown skin to best effect and logged into Skype to call their loved ones back home. Last but not least they called my computer, onto which their orange faces – one smiling (Mum), one not – would manifest like a pair of radioactive kumquats. A disjointed exchange would follow, generally concluding with a discussion about Nick's overall suitability. If this got out of hand, I could pretend we'd been cut off. That was the beauty of technology: you could blame almost anything on it.

Over the past year, as they'd gradually accepted I'd be sticking with Nick, and that he probably wasn't so bad after all, the focus of disappointment became the wedding itself. No date had been set, and, after I'd warned my parents that I probably wouldn't be walking up the aisle in Westminster Abbey swaddled in tulle while Lesley Garrett yelled arias at the altar, the folks made it clear they were not impressed. So much for just wanting me to be happy; what they wanted, in all honesty, was to be shown a damn good, preferably very expensive time. When it became apparent this dream was in jeopardy, they blamed their future son-in-law for being a skinflint, even though I too was keen to keep things low-key. There's something about being involved with the staging of big, full-on shows night after night that makes the idea of scaling things back quite appealing.

Actually, I wouldn't have minded just running off and doing it in secret somewhere, and it was a plan Nick would definitely be up for, but the Concierge camp would never forgive us if they received an email out of the blue bearing the words "We did it!" underneath a picture of the happy couple, happy partly because we were miles away from our insane loved ones. Anyway, Concierge had seen enough divorces over the years. They were ready for a wedding, and even if it wasn't going to rival Elton John and David Furnish's big day, they wanted to be invited, they wanted to hear the vows and they wanted to eat the cake. This was all well and good, but so far, I'd planned nothing at all. Things kept getting in the way, although I couldn't work out what these 'things' were, when I tried to pin myself down about it. The whole concept just seemed increasingly remote. A bit like Nick. I stared at the little star on my ring finger and didn't know what to feel.

I wandered into the kitchen and topped up my tea. I'd had a troubled night's sleep and I still hadn't replied to Nick. Almost as soon as I thought of him, my mobile beeped. This sort of thing happened a lot. We seemed to be synched up, which made the difficult patches and silences all the more confusing – it should have been easier than this. 'You OK? Betty said she'd seen you. I'll be in after 6pm. Stay over? X'

'Don't worry,' I texted back. 'Just tired. Maybe see you Sunday.'

I sipped the tea and ran a hand over the worn spines of my vinyl collection, pulling out the old faithful, *Marquee Moon*. This album was getting a lot of attention at the moment, which could only mean one thing: I was feeling fragile. I gently lowered the needle onto track six, side two. 'Guiding Light'. The opening notes rang out and the sound filled my head with colour and light, pale blue, pink and gold; it was like this bunch of New York reprobates had accidentally conjured up the colour of heaven. I could almost feel the connection between myself and Nick strengthen just by listening. *Marquee Moon* was the bridge. I closed my eyes for a moment. By the time 'Friction' had kicked in, the phone was ringing and the bubble had burst. Betty.

"Come to the front door! I didn't want to knock in case it reminded you of that tapping." Bless her. Underneath all the bluster and hocus-pocus, Betty had a heart of gold. She kissed me on the cheek before whirling into the living room.

"Drink?"

"Green tea, please. I've already had about a gallon of coffee at Nick's this morning," said Betty, eyes sparkling. "I didn't hear any weird noises while I was there – well, other than Nick talking – but it's all on for tomorrow night. We've got the place to ourselves."

"Yay," I said weakly.

"But enough about that," continued Betty. "Guess who I met? Guess. Come on!" She sat forward, waiting like an excited poodle. "Never mind, can't wait. I met Sam." She raised a pencilled eyebrow and did a little jiggle, causing her collection of bangles to rattle like sleigh-bells.

"Who's Sam?"

"Sam!" repeated Betty at an even greater volume, as if shouting would assist me in working out who he was. "New roadie. He's the replacement for Dogfish after what happened with the— "

"I don't need to hear the Dogfish story again," I interrupted, trying not to heave at the memory. You don't want to know.

Betty snorted in agreement. "Horrible. The worst thing about it was the— "

"NO! I mean it. Anyway, go on, you're dying to tell me about Sam. Distinguished older gent?" I realised this was wishful thinking and that he was probably about thirty-six.

"Probably about thirty-six," shrugged Betty. "Ten years age difference isn't too bad." And the rest. "Anyway, he's very friendly, he's got lovely wavy blond hair and one of those nice faces," Betty continued impishly, blowing on her tea.

"Sounds like a Golden Retriever. How's Nick?"

"Didn't look good, actually. Tired, unkempt, kind of… blue."

"Blue?"

"More colourless, really. Bit moody. I think I'd woken him up before he'd managed to get his full fifteen hours. Are you making sure he eats properly and takes supplements and whatnot? He takes care of that hound better than he looks after himself."

"He's a grown man."

"What about Jo Wood?" said Betty. "Travelled everywhere with Ronnie with a portable stove so she could cook organic meals for him wherever they were. Queen of the art of rock star maintenance," she concluded respectfully.

"And look what happened. Men don't want to be pampered like giant babies – well, apart from Gomez. It's emasculating."

Betty shook her head with an air of condescension and leaned back, stretching out her hands in front of her to admire her rings.

"SHITBAGS!" she yelled. "My ring. The topaz. I put it on this morning and now it's gone." She got up and started prodding at cushions, scouring the floor and retracing her steps back out of the room and up the front path. Fortunately the ring was the size of a meteor and wouldn't be hard to spot.

"Did you take it off at Nick's?" I called as Betty scrabbled around in her MG. She paused. Yes. It had to be there. She remembered twisting it and slipping it on and off when she was nervous. She leapt into the car and started the ignition, shouting through the open window, "I'll see you tomorrow night. Pip pip!" And she was off, hurtling to Richmond, bringing up Nick's number on her satnav and calling his landline. It went straight to his answering service.

Betty pulled into the drive, empty other than a rich carpet of red and orange leaves and spiky sweet chestnuts. Fumbling in her carpet-bag for the keys he'd given her, Betty worked out what went where and let herself in. Within seconds of closing the door, she became aware of a tapping sound, increasing in volume. She froze, squeezing her eyes shut. When the noise stopped and was replaced by quiet snuffling, Betty opened her eyes and looked down. Brando.

"Christ on a bike," she breathed, bending down and stroking a velvety ear. Her quartz pendant bashed him gently on the head, prompting him to bumble off, wheezing and clattering through the dog-flap. It was true. Nick's house was not the sort of place you wanted to be alone in, Brando or no Brando. If the real Brando was there, well, that would be different.

"Nick?" No response. Betty wasn't sure why she'd even bothered calling her brother's name – his car wasn't outside, he was clearly out – but it felt like the right thing to do. Betty took a deep breath and walked quickly into the kitchen. There was the ring, gleaming on the worktop next to *Synth Quarterly*. She squeezed it back on and hurried straight back to the front door. Between the clacks of her heels, she heard a groaning floorboard, followed by the thud of something heavy slumping against a door. Betty felt a cold rush of fear.

She slammed the front door behind her and, with a great deal of crashing and blaspheming, tried to remember which keys went into which locks. That was it, she thought as she threw herself into the leather-scented safety of her car. She'd heard it for herself. It couldn't have been an intruder, the house was like Fort Knox. Betty felt a thrill in her stomach as she wiped her clammy hands on her trousers and backed out of the drive.

"Betty!" It was Sam, pulling up to the forecourt in Nick's Citroën. There was no sign of its owner, unless he'd fallen asleep in the back, which was not out of the question. Betty stopped and opened the window. "What are you doing with Nick's car?"

"Had some problems with my brakes. The AA picked the van up," he said. "Nick let me use the car. I didn't need much space for his gear anyway." He scanned her face. "You all right?"

Betty opened her mouth to speak and then paused. "And… Nick?"

"Said he was going for a walk. Lovely day for it."

Betty gave a forced little smile and drove on. She looked out for Nick as she passed the deer park. What was the point of having a dog if you were going to go walking without it? Betty jabbed at her phone as she drove, clicking on the 'voice text' option. "Sylvie, am on my way back to yours," she intoned slowly, the letters appearing obediently on the screen. "I hope you have alcohol."

Les Tanner was pacing around his office, tutting and rubbing his bald head. Les was not the most relaxed individual thanks to years managing Concierge, and he was prone to outbursts of violent anger, which was useful when it came to promoters who wouldn't pay or persistent berks who sneaked backstage, but not good for his blood pressure. Still, living healthily to a ripe old age is rarely the top priority when one chooses a life in the music business. "Unless you're Travis, or Coldplay," Les would smirk in response to any concerns voiced over his lifestyle, his weight, the veins that stood out in his forehead. "Granola rockers." The words would be spat out like bitter little seeds. The kind of seeds one might find in one's granola, indeed.

Les avoided Concierge rehearsals if he could help it, but today he was making an exception. He had some good news, some not so good news and some highly irregular and possibly very bad news. All of this had to be handled face-to-face.

That morning, Les had staggered downstairs to find a blank postcard on his door-mat with just one word on the back: 'Arseholes'. It was spelt in cut-out newspaper letters, ransom-note style, and the card bore a Norwich postmark. Les didn't know anyone in Norwich other than his Aunt Clarice. He was fairly confident he could rule her out.

On phoning Johnson Large that day, he ascertained that he too had received a cryptic postcard with the word 'I've' on the back. Birmingham postmark. "Bring it to the rehearsal," said Les. "I'd better ring the others." He left a message for Nick and texted Abra, asking her to bring her post with her. Gomez was exfoliating in the bath when Les called.

"Phone!" Gomez screamed. Pearl dutifully brought his mobile into the bathroom. "It's Les," she whispered, with her hand over the mouthpiece.

"Hold it to my ear then," Gomez snapped. "Mind the hair. Yes? I'm in the bath so make it quick."

Les didn't want to know. "I'm coming to rehearsal later as I've got news for you all. And this may sound strange but I need you to bring today's mail with you. I'll explain later. Just make sure you bring any *mail* to the *rehearsal*," he repeated, emphasising the important words in the hope that it might make a difference.

Gomez put the phone on speakerphone for Pearl's benefit. "Pearl, you deal with this."

"OK. Pearl, I need to see any mail that Gomez received today," repeated Les patiently. "Particularly if it's a postcard."

"Right." Pearl trotted downstairs as fast as her tightly-skirted haunches could carry her. None of them received much post at the house as most of it ended up in a PO Box. Due to the price of fame, there weren't many people who knew Gomez's address. But tucked between the takeaway flyers and the parish magazine, there it was. A postcard, blank on one side, but with the word 'Come' emblazoned on the other, rubber-stamped in red ink. Pearl checked the postmark. Cardiff. She only really knew one person in Cardiff: Carly Davies, Gomez's unstable ex-girlfriend.

Gomez dumped Carly two years ago as she couldn't cope with the communal lifestyle he led with his other partners. For some reason, she wanted Gomez to herself or not at all. Gomez went for the 'not at all' option, not least because he'd noticed Carly and Johnson stumbling off together one night after a gig. It was possibly entirely for Gomez's benefit from Carly's point of view, but he wrote her off that night on the grounds of her being 'promiscuous'. Double standards and rock 'n' roll are great bedfellows.

Carly took it badly, turning up at gigs to throw missiles at Gomez from the front row, phoning up Les to try to keep tabs on her ex, and finally, selling her story to the *Sunday Sport*. It was a lurid feature crammed with tales of mind-boggling sexual adventures and pictures of a blow-dried Carly wearing Janet Reger underwear and an injured expression. Gomez took the whole thing as a great compliment to his prowess. When Les assured him few people actually read the *Sport*, he was quite disappointed.

Pearl slipped the postcard into Gomez's leather man-bag. "Done it!" she called up the stairs. "She's done it," Gomez shouted at the phone, which was now sitting on the side of the bath next to a bottle of conditioner.

"Good," said Les. He hung up and picked up his card again. The word 'Arseholes' glared back at him. Les shook his head and headed out to the car.

*

It was 6pm, and everyone had finally arrived at Johnson's studio after being called for 4pm. Les always called them too early, that way he knew he'd have the full complement by the time he actually wanted them.

"OK," said Les, regarding the various Concierge members, draped over settees and leaning against speakers. "I've got news."

"You're finally getting that hair transplant?" offered Johnson, munching popcorn from a bag.

"No, thank you Johnson, I am not. I'd like you to keep any contributions to yourself until I have finished, if you would be so kind." Gomez and Johnson caught each other's eye. They knew the more polite Les was, the more likely it was that he would self-combust at any moment.

"As I was saying, I have news. Firstly, Nick, you need to call Gary Numan back, he's been trying to get hold of you for ages now. He's starting to take offence."

"Probably just wants to know what hair-dye he uses," Johnson whispered.

"So he can avoid it," Gomez whispered back before thrusting his hand into the bag of popcorn and throwing a fistful of kernels at his face. Only about five succeeded in making it into his open mouth.

"Secondly," Les continued, "we have another UK tour booked. October to December. There are a few dates on the Continent too. Nick, are you… is he snoring? He's asleep! He's actually fallen asleep! Already!" Abra elbowed Nick in the ribs, causing his eyes to slowly open. No other part of his body moved.

"What did I just say?" said Les through his teeth.

"Something about a hair transplant?" murmured Nick. The room collapsed into muted laughter. Abra rolled her eyes and started chopping out lines of Colombia's finest on Johnson's coffee table.

"No." Les rubbed his face hard. "I said we have another UK tour booked, October to December, AND," he crescendoed, his face turning an unhealthy colour, "A FEW DATES ON THE CONTINENT."

"Oh, good," said Nick drowsily.

"Who's the promoter?" asked Gomez. Les looked uncomfortable.

"That's the other thing I wanted to talk to you about," he said. "It's Rick Bird."

"Rip-off Rick?" said Johnson. "Bird the Bastard? Tell me you're joking."

Les was prepared for this reaction, but there was little else on the table that offered the kind of money Concierge were accustomed to. "I'm hoping it will be more a case of Rick the Reformed Character."

Gomez sniffed. "So you said yes to Rip-off Rick?"

"What did you expect me to do? Do you have any other ideas?" Les brought a fist down onto a speaker, causing Johnson to turn white. Gomez pouted. Pearl and Ange weren't there to protect him.

"What was the other thing?" asked Abra quickly, feeling that a change in subject might be prudent. "The mail thing? I brought mine. I haven't even looked at it yet, just brought everything." She opened up her sequinned bag and emptied a small pile of post onto the table, carefully avoiding the neat little slashes of powder in front of her.

"Good," said Les, calming down slightly. "And the rest of you? Nick? I left you a message; did you bring your mail? The correct answer is yes. Just say yes."

"No."

"Jesus! What's the matter with you tonight?"

"Don't have a cow, Les," Nick yawned, fumbling for his phone. "Betty's at home looking after Brando. I'll call and get her to take a look."

"Oh *thank you*," fumed Les, turning away and doing the breathing exercises his therapist had recommended. Nick stared at his phone for some time, his index finger hovering indecisively over the keypad.

"Does anyone, erm… know my number?"

"JESUS!" Les shrieked again, his hands clapped to his gleaming head. "It's like being hand-cuffed to idiots." Johnson hurriedly dialled Nick's number on his own phone and handed it to him, keen to protect his studio from Les's fists.

After some mumbling from Nick and many exchanged glances, he handed the phone back.

"Well?" said Les.

"Bank statement, copy of *MOJO*, blank postcard."

Les's eyes glinted. "Right! Blank postcard. Now I want you all to look through your post. Both Johnson and I also received blank postcards today with just one word on them. Johnson's has the word 'I've' written on there, and my one bears the word… well, 'arseholes'."

Everyone dissolved into mirth again.

"Shut it," growled Les. "Twats."

"Arseholes… wasn't that the name of that band you used to be in, Johnson?" asked Abra. Nick stifled a laugh.

"No," said Johnson. 'We were called 'Arse?' With a question mark."

Gomez, still sulking, pulled out his postcard and slapped it onto the table.

"Someone's trying to send us a message, and it's not just going to be 'I've arseholes'. For lots of reasons," said Les.

"Mine says 'back' written in lipstick," said Abra.

"Someone had written the word 'you' on mine, apparently," added Nick.

"Guess what mine says?" giggled Gomez. "'Come'. Haha! Come!"

"Grow up," said Les. "Put them all on the table. Right. 'I've Arseholes You Back Come'. OK, so it's not that."

"That's something I haven't tried yet," said Gomez.

Les glared. "I don't even know what you mean by that, but I do know you're being disgusting. Save it."

"I've… come… back… you… arseholes," said Nick, rearranging the cards. "Hm. Er… Oh dear."

"Who has come back?" said Les. "Who would go to the trouble of doing something like this?"

Nobody spoke. "I need a cigarette," said Les. "I don't like this at all. And you lot had better get rehearsing. You've got a charity gig and a tour to work up to, and I don't wish to hear the same set as last time."

"What?" squeaked Gomez. "You expect us to go straight into rehearsing after all that? I need a drink."

"Just get it together. I'm going home." Les pulled on his

Crombie and strode out as Concierge started setting up, all trying to work out who might have sent the message, who had come back… and who thought they were arseholes? The latter question was the hardest to answer; it really could have been almost anyone.

Before they could even get onto the usual business of slagging off Les as soon as he was out of the room, the door crashed open again. He was back, ashen and wide-eyed, leaning dramatically against the door-frame.

"Speak!" demanded Gomez.

Johnson approached Les cautiously and sat him back down on the sofa. "Look," he stammered. "Look at this. It was on the front step." Les sank his head into one shaking hand and with the other passed a brown-paper package up to Johnson.

"It stinks!" said Johnson, recoiling.

"Just open it," said Les. He delicately obeyed, as if he thought it was about to blow up. Then he laughed.

"It's a load of empty fag packets and cigarette butts! Probably just fell out of the bin," said Johnson. "Bloody hell, Les, you need a holiday."

Les glanced up at him. "The bag is addressed to 'Concierge', spelt in letters cut out FROM A NEWSPAPER. Look at it. Tell me what you are looking at?"

Johnson paused. "Some cigarette packets?"

"Well done, yes, well done. But they're Benson and Hedges packets, aren't they? Benson. And Hedges. You know what this means, don't you?"

"Oh God," said Nick, flopping face-first onto the chaise longue.

"That's right," replied Les. "Now we're just waiting for Little and Large to catch up," he added, looking at Gomez and Johnson impatiently. "Abra, no disrespect but I don't expect you to get it, and before you hit me it's because this concerns someone you've never met, lucky bloody you. Anyway, chaps, in your own time.

Benson and Hedges? 'I've come back, you arseholes'? Do you really have no idea?"

The penny dropped. "OH GOD, NO!" shouted Gomez, clutching handfuls of hair. He was on the verge of a full-scale panic attack. Johnson saw this as a golden opportunity to legitimately smack him in the face.

"Yes," said Les. "Henson mother-fucking Bedges. Disappeared over fifteen years ago, not a word from him since, not even to chase royalties. And now he's back."

Johnson and Gomez slowly sat down either side of him. Nick remained face-down and motionless.

"This is horrible," said Johnson, staring into space. "Was there anyone outside when you saw the package?"

"No. I doubt it would have been him dropping it off though. All those cards have got different postmarks on them; you don't think he went to the trouble of going to those places himself? Oh no, not Bedges. Lazy bastard. He's got people working for him. Probably some nitwit fans he has in his thrall, they always go for the unpredictable ones. He's been waiting for us to enjoy a comeback and now he's trying to ruin it. RUIN IT!"

"Calm down, Les," said Abra, handing him a mug of whisky. "Anyway, I thought he died? When I got the job, I distinctly remember you saying I was replacing Henson Bedges who, I quote: 'tragically set fire to himself'. So what, he's risen from the dead?"

"No. I mean, yes, he did set fire to himself. On numerous occasions actually."

"I set fire to him once, too," interjected Johnson.

"Ah yes, I remember that," said Les, smiling fondly at the memory. "But no, he's not actually dead. Just dead to us. Well, to be fair, we did think he was dead at first after the fire – it all went quiet and then his mother released a selection of his 'solo work' under the title *I'm Dead – How Are You?* to make a bit of cash. But it turned out he was alive and well. Anyway, the main thing is, the 'dead' thing kind of worked for us. We were hoping never to see him again. He made our lives a misery; fucking awful bass-player too. We were just too scared to sack him – he's a nutcase. Homicidal maniac. Pyromaniac. Narcomaniac."

"Megalomaniac," contributed Gomez.

"Takes one to know one."

"I heard that, Nick."

"Bibliomaniac," offered Johnson.

Les looked at him. "Bibliomaniac? He could barely read a set-list."

"I was… just trying to think of different kinds of maniacs," said Johnson quietly.

"The point is," concluded Les, "we do not want him anywhere near us. Anyone who has any contact with him or even has an inkling that he is around must come to me."

Abra scrunched up her nose against the smell of stale cigarettes. "You'll have to remind me what he looks like," she said.

"You'll smell him before you see him," warned Les. "A cross between charred hair, fags and cheese toasties, with a top-note of B.O."

Nick dragged himself up to a seated position like a sleepy wolf and reached under the table, lifting out a pile of old LPs. "Knock yourself out," he said, shoving them towards Abra. "These should familiarise you with his diverse range of facial expressions." Henson only had one expression: a weird combination of annoyance and glee. Not a face you would forget in a hurry; similarly, it was not a face you wanted to see more than once if you could help it.

"Oh," said Abra. "I see."

"Exactly," said Les. "But don't worry, there is no way that he is going to return to Concierge, absolutely no way."

"I'm not worried," she replied steadily. "I studied ju-jitsu when I was a teenager. I can make him lose consciousness or shit himself with one well-judged chop on the right pressure point. And that's just for starters."

"Er, hello?" said Johnson. "What if he comes at you with one of his flame-throwers? Good luck with that."

"Maybe Sylvie could knock up some fire-proof outfits for the tour?" suggested Gomez.

"Shut up, both of you. Although seriously, Abra, maybe you should speak to Sylvie… "

She pulled a face. "Jog on. Sylvie's got enough to think about with Nick… " She bit her lip, having stopped herself just that little bit too late.

"Go on," said Nick, dark eyes widening.

Everyone looked at Abra. "I'm just going to, erm…" said Johnson, shuffling off.

"Me too," said Gomez quickly, disappearing into the other room with Johnson.

"What?" repeated Nick, straightening up.

"Nothing. Just wedding stuff, it's stressful. Don't worry about it. She hasn't said anything, it's not like she's got cold feet."

She was protesting too much. The words *She's terrified because your house is freaky which means there's no way she's going to want to live there and it doesn't help that you keep bloody disappearing*, circled her mind like a goldfish on speed.

Nick looked at her without blinking for an unfeasibly long time. She smiled uneasily, her shoulders gradually reaching her ears with tension. "Honestly, it's fine! I saw her the other night, she couldn't have been more excited, despite the… despite the…"

"Despite the… " prompted Nick, staring at her like a basilisk.

"Fuck's sake, Nick, you're making her nervous, just leave it," said Les. "You're making me nervous. You make everybody nervous. Is it any surprise that Sylvie is nervous about doing the most nerve-wracking thing in the world with the man who makes everyone nervous? Now the word 'nervous' sounds weird."

"Despite the… " repeated Nick.

"Despite the… stress… of organising the wedding! It's

probably her parents putting pressure on, you know what they're like," said Abra, beads of sweat forming on her lip.

Nick rose wordlessly and walked off.

"What have you done?" whispered Les. "We need him on form."

Abra grabbed the mug of whisky she'd given to him earlier. "Piss off, Les."

"Seriously, I cannot have anyone getting Nick's dander up before this tour. Once he goes peculiar, that's it."

"I said, piss off! It's fine."

"Right," said Les, getting up. "Off I piss. You'd better put all this aside. That charity gig is in one week. If you can, try to put Henson Bedges to the back of your mind. I'll take care of him."

Abra threw a cushion at the back of his head as he left. Henson Bedges was already at the back of her mind until Les dragged him to the front of it again.

"What is going on?" said Johnson, poking his head round the door. "What's with the tension? I don't think I can deal with much more of it."

"Full moon," replied Gomez.

"In Scorpio," added Abra, glancing through the window. The moon was too high to be seen, but it was making its presence very much felt. The Coven-members were embarking on Operation Nick's House right at that very moment. "Insane," she muttered, imagining the kind of spirit-bothering scenes that would put Madame Blavatsky to shame. "Everybody's gone insane."

"It's cold in here, I don't like it," grimaced Pearl, rubbing her arms and looking around the gloomy entrance hall.

"Shouldn't have worn that, then," replied Betty, casting an eye over Pearl's skimpy ensemble and throwing her a pashmina. Fortified by the presence of the others, she shepherded everyone into the lounge.

The entire Coven, minus Abra, had descended on Nick's house, peering about like wary cats, arms folded against the chill, chattering quietly. Betty had arrived early to arrange candles, meditate and spritz the lounge, where the séance was to be held, with a blend of essential oils and sea salt, mixed specifically for this occasion.

Betty and I had turned up together, neither of us wanting to arrive alone. I'd walked Brando and put him to bed in the kitchen with his favourite dog therapy CD, *Classics for Canines*, playing nearby. Everything was ready. I wasn't exactly sure what for, but Betty would take care of that.

"Behold!" exclaimed the hostess, gesturing to the coffee table which was festooned with Waitrose finger food and glasses of red wine. "And before you ask, no, I didn't cook any of it." Everyone ventured forth to peruse the spread, and Pearl started unwrapping an unusually shaped object.

"And what the hell is that?" Betty demanded.

"I made a cake for the occasion. You said it was the full moon, so I thought, you know, 'moon'... "

"I see." Betty looked at the offending article, a Victoria sponge baked in the shape of a pair of buttocks. There was certainly plenty to go around but it didn't really chime with the sense of gravitas Betty was trying to maintain.

"Anyway," she said. "Help yourselves and try to relax." Ange automatically reached into her bag for Rizlas and a little tin of grass. "But no drugs," added Betty hastily. "Any vibrations of paranoia or confusion might attract lower energies." No one said anything. There wasn't really an answer to that.

"It's cold," repeated Pearl. Ange nodded in vigorous agreement. I tried out my best reassuring smile and turned up the elderly radiators as Pearl arranged herself on Nick's worn sofa. "It's probably cold because of the... well, you know."

I sat down opposite Betty and pressed a finger into the warm wax of a tea-light that had gone out of its own accord. "I still don't know how tonight is going to work, Bet. What's going to happen?"

"That's the thing. You never really know."

"What happened the last time you held one?"

Betty hesitated. "To be honest, I was more of an observer."

"Closer than any of us have ever been. Go on," urged Ange.

"Well, it was a long time ago, but everyone sat at the table and joined hands. I remember this strange presence entering the room, and cutting a long story short, the information the spirit came forward with helped to solve a murder." She gathered pace, the Coven-members were in the palm of her hand. "It was in this funny little cottage in a village called Summer something. Middle Summer. I must have been visiting someone there. Anyway I distinctly recall— "

Ange butted in. "A commercial break? This was on *Midsomer Murders*, wasn't it? You saw it on the bleeding telly."

There was only so much of Betty's fantastical approach to life I could take and this was definitely the limit. "So," I said. "We are about to hold a séance led by someone whose only previous experience of séances is seeing one on the TV?" Betty picked up a piece of lettuce from her plate and shoved it into her mouth. When she had finally finished chewing, taking a moment to check her teeth in the back of a spoon, she spoke.

"You don't want the séance, is that what you're saying?"

"Yes. I mean, no, I don't want the séance. Oh, I don't know, Betty, all I know is that I heard something and so did you. I appreciate you trying but I don't want to stir things up, especially if no one actually knows what they're doing anyway."

"Why don't we just sit here and listen?" suggested Pearl, twisting her necklace around her fingers. "If we do hear something, we'd know we weren't imagining it – we'd have witnesses."

It was agreed that this was the most sensible course of action, and everyone made themselves comfortable. I decided we might need more alcohol as the night wore on, and Pearl accompanied me to the kitchen for more provisions, largely because she knew I didn't want to go anywhere alone in that house any more.

"I know what you mean about this place," said Pearl, addressing the back of my head as I searched the cupboards. "It's incredible but… well, I don't know about ghosts, but it just feels sort of sad."

"I know. But Nick loves it, it's almost part of him now."

"What's going to happen when you get married? You don't want to live here. I couldn't live here." I'd asked myself this question more than once; it couldn't be ignored. I knew full well Nick had no intention of leaving this place. In his eyes, it was the ideal marital home and, on paper, it sort of was. I didn't want to tear him away from the one place that represented stability for him. But there were my feelings to consider. I still wasn't convinced I could get used to being the lady of this particular manor; it would be easier to imagine the future at all if Nick wasn't becoming even more of an island.

Tim Burton and Helena Bonham-Carter had the right idea. Technically living in two separate houses, but next door to each other. I'd often wondered whether there was some way of adapting this. Maybe we could keep our respective houses but build some kind of underground tunnel between the two. But no, Nick and I would just have to get on the same page, which ought to be at least slightly easier than single-handedly digging a tunnel between Strawberry Hill and Richmond without getting in the way of various plague pits.

"Right, everyone," announced Betty, taking charge again with enforced bravery. "Once we've got everything we need, we must choose our corner, get comfy and listen. It could be rather Zen-like, like meditating, only more stressful, and, erm… well, potentially quite frightening. But no, it's going to be fine, we're here to help Sylvie."

"And because you couldn't resist a bit of drama," said Ange.

"And because that's what friends are for. Family almost," she twinkled at me.

We settled into silence. Every noise leapt out at us: the ticking clock over the gaping black fireplace, the occasional creak of the baby grand as the room warmed up, the clanking of the radiators, the cry of a peacock ringing out from the park – that one was especially unpopular. But after almost forty-five minutes in silence (miraculous given who was present), none of us had heard what we'd been listening out for. We didn't know whether to be relieved or disappointed.

"Time for a coffee break?" I suggested, looking at my watch. It was getting on for 9pm and I wanted to break the spell before the clock chimed and made everyone jump out of their skins. There was a bustle of grateful movement as the Coven-members variously stretched their legs and peeked out of the window at the moon, beaming down like a spotlight. Before long the room was alive with noise again, but, given the nature of the evening, the usual gossip-fest was eschewed in favour of The Big Questions. I made for the kitchen as the Coven commenced discussing the spirit world – did they really believe? (Pearl: "Absolutely." Ange: "Fuck off.") Astrology – is there anything in it? (Betty: "It's a science like any other." Ange: "Load of bollocks.") And eventually, God – male or female? (Pearl: "Female." Ange: "Facial hair? Menopause? The bastard's a dude, all right.")

I spooned instant coffee into mugs, head fuzzy from wine and anxiety. Brando was growling quietly in his sleep. I could see the moonlight shining on the lawn outside, bouncing off the luminescent bark of the birches. I didn't want to look for too long. I didn't know what I might see.

Betty rushed in, making me start. "Sorry. Bit on edge myself. *Christ*!" Betty shrieked as if to prove her point, toppling backwards. "It's OK, it's just my phone! Abra. Probably checking to see how we're getting on." This was doing me no good at all.

"Hello?" Betty squawked. "How are things? You what? SHIT." Betty ran back into the lounge. "ABORT! You need to get out of here, all of you. Nick is already on his way back. Sylvie, you can stay, it's not out of the question that you'd be here to keep me company."

"No," I said, a little too forcefully. "He asked me to stay last night and I said no. It won't look great that I came over when he wasn't here. And Betty," I accelerated my appeal before she had a chance to interject. "If I'm here when he gets back he's going to expect me to stay the night and I *cannot* stay the night." I tried to slow down but it was all coming out at speed. Everything I'd wanted to say was ready to be heard, whether I liked it or not. "I'm trying to be cool about everything but it's not like before. It's like he's always somewhere else. I don't know, sometimes I wonder whether he might be cheating. I know you're going to defend him but what am I supposed to think?"

"Sylvie, he's got his faults but he has never been like that," said Betty. "For one thing, he's a Taurus with Taurus rising. Moody bastard, yes, but solid as a rock. Talk to him. Maybe not about the paranormal stuff. Just anything, the wedding, anything. He'll come out of himself when you do. You can't just avoid him just because of the house, he won't understand."

"*I* don't understand," I whispered. Betty hugged me, not knowing what to say. "We'll head off," called Pearl through the kitchen door. She gave me a sympathetic look, a look I was already getting sick of, and the pair of them tottered out into the drive. I took one last look around for anything incriminating before pulling on my coat, shivering against the cold satin lining.

"I think Brando's CD is stuck, Betty. It's starting to sound a bit Steve Reich," I said, flicking my hair out from under my scarf. "Are you going to be all right here on your own?"

Betty patted her crimson hair and gave a tumbling laugh, which meant she was absolutely not all right there on her own.

"It's only an hour! Then Nick'll be back," she said through clenched teeth, giving me another fragrant hug. "Go home. We'll get to the bottom of this." I blew her a kiss and drove into the leafy darkness.

Betty locked the door, turned off *Classics for Canines* and switched on Radio 2 for a change of ambience. Chuck Berry burst out of the speaker. 'Little Queenie'. That would raise the vibrations nicely, and that was especially necessary, given that she was now going on a little treasure hunt. She'd have to be fast, but she knew exactly what she was looking for. Little boxes crammed with secrets, powder, needles … Part of the habit for Nick was the ritual, the elevating of the entire process into an aesthetic, almost religious ceremony. But every cupboard and drawer simply gazed back at her with perfect innocence. Nothing to see.

There wasn't time to launch a full-scale search and have everything looking exactly as Nick had left it by the time he came back, so Betty took her coffee into the lounge and plumped the cushions on the sofa. By the time Nick arrived he found his sister seated in the lotus position on the floor, chanting furiously.

"Good evening," he said with quiet amusement. Betty screeched at the sight of the dark figure in the doorway.

"NEVER do that. I was chanting."

"I noticed," said Nick, taking off his coat and flinging it over a chair. "How's Brando?"

"Oh, fine," Betty said, getting up and brushing down her clothes. "Sylvie put his CD on for him and he went out like a light."

"Sylvie?" said Nick. Balls. Betty wanted to disappear. "Er, yes. She wanted to see you. That's why she came; she forgot you had a rehearsal." Betty was not giving a convincing performance, but she continued, babbling. "She left because I told her you wouldn't be back until tomorrow."

His lips curled into a sarcastic smile. "No. She doesn't want to see me. But you knew that already, I suppose? She talks to you. She obviously talks to Abra."

"She'd talk to you if you were more communicative," said Betty, her eyes narrowing. "Look, I know I brought this up before, but you're not... "

"Please not this again."

"Well, what is going on? You're not seeing someone else, are you?"

"What?" said Nick. "That's insane. You know how much I... "

"Of course I know. *I* know," she added pointedly. "Anyway, you couldn't."

"No." He took out a cigarette and lit it. "Hang on, what do you mean I couldn't?"

Betty sighed. "I mean, you couldn't. Not with the truckloads of Taurus you've got jamming up your birth-chart. I don't mean you physically couldn't, I just... "

"OK. But the point is it's Sylvie who doesn't want to see me."

Betty leant forward. "She loves you. She's just a little freaked out because you're acting weird. I mean, you really are behaving as if you were back on the— "

"I just need time to regroup," he murmured, shrugging off the conversation. "Anyway, we're going back on tour in October. The promoter's Rick Bird, so we'll have to wear stab-proof vests, but…"

"Bird the bastard?"

"Yes, Bird the fucking bastard!" He didn't want another conversation about Rick Bird tonight, although to be fair, he hadn't really taken part in the first one.

"Out of interest," said Betty, "what did Abra say to you?"

"Not much. She started talking about Sylvie and then stopped herself, made some excuse about wedding stress. I'm not buying that. We've agreed to keep it low-key and she hasn't even organised anything yet; what's to be stressed about? Abra said her parents might be pressurising her, but I don't know. "

Nick walked into the kitchen, tuning the radio back to 3. "What's with all the cups with coffee in them?" he called. Betty swore under her breath.

"I was doing an experiment. Like tea-leaf-reading but with coffee granules." Bollocks, she thought. He is going to know that's bollocks. Everyone knows you read coffee grounds, not granules.

"Right," said Nick, too poleaxed to question further. He picked up a mug and poured hot water into it. Betty joined him in the kitchen.

"Anyway, you're back early," she said, trying to sound casual.

"Difficult night. Henson Bedges is back."

"You're joking."

Nick stirred his coffee. "Les is worried about him turning up on tour with his matches."

"Shall I perform a protection rite?"

Nick smiled. "It'll take more than that to stop Bedges. Look, why don't you go home before it gets too late? I need an early night."

She looked at him. "An early night? You?"

"Yes, me. I'm tired."

Betty collected her things and kissed her brother. "I can see that," she said, taking in his grey-white skin, the dark rings around his eyes. "Take some vitamins, Herman Munster. Get a suntan. And will you please try to communicate with Sylvie?"

"I am trying," he protested.

"I mean with words," she said, heading towards her car in the glare of the security light. "Sentences. Out loud. And to her face. Don't forget to listen as well. It'll help, I promise."

Everyone in the Concierge camp had their rituals. Some really were rituals, like Betty and her amateur spell-casting. Johnson's pre-gig routine included shouting affirmations at himself in the mirror. Then there was Gomez and his harem. Their rituals were definitely the most interesting.

My favourite ritual wasn't quite as exciting as the others', but every Sunday I went to Bluebell's Diner, a café two minutes from my door. I would then sit in a dark corner at the back and order a cup of coffee that was bigger than my head. Once fortified, I would then walk to the flea market and hunt for scraps and swatches, buttons and beads, old patterns and maps and anything else that took my fancy, and a happy day of collaging would usually follow. I didn't have the patience to meditate but this was the next best thing, as far as I was concerned.

Bluebell's was just on the right side of trendy and I didn't even mind that I always seemed to smell of cooking oil when I left. The fact the staff gave out free bowls of popcorn made up for that, and they had a big, shining jukebox packed with singles by Howlin' Wolf, Chubby Checker, Buddy Holly, Louis Prima… All the good stuff. I made the commitment to get up early so I could pick a tune and bag 'my' table as the rest of the Strawberry Hill bourgeoisie were still emerging from their Egyptian cotton sheets.

But this time, as I walked automatically towards my favourite table, a waitress with a platinum beehive stopped me in my tracks.

"Hiyaaa! Would you like to take a seat over here?" she chirruped, gesturing to a table in the window. Not ideal. Broke the ritual. Bit glary, but I was too groggy to care. I had my Aviators on anyway.

"Sylvie!" I looked back towards my usual gloomy spot to see a towering vision of huge hair, false eyelashes and an all-in-one outfit that seemed to glow in the relative darkness. It was Abra, sitting at my table. She'd been waiting for me. I navigated my way around the pushchairs and barstools and exuberant waiting staff. I wondered whether this was her usual Sunday attire or whether she was still wearing it from the night before. "Nice lipstick."

"Lip-stain," she corrected. "It's an Anna Sui blackberry lip-stain. But thanks. Now, I wanted to talk to you. Have you spoken to Nick?"

"Oh God, what now?"

Abra took a gulp of milkshake. "I didn't mean to, but last night… well, it was an accident, but… "

"Go on." My eyes bored into hers like a cobra and Abra twisted her napkin. "Did Nick teach you how to do that? Undisputed master of the cold, hard stare."

"Go on," I repeated. I guess I had learned a thing or two from Nick.

"OK. I sort of let slip that you were feeling… a bit funny… about things. I didn't say anything about the… you know, ghost thing. I just covered it up, made out like you were getting nervous about the wedding. Stop looking at me like that!"

"Why did you do that? I don't want him to think that! I'm already on the back-foot with him as it is." I hid briefly behind my coffee. Why had I allowed myself to be steamrollered into telling the entire Coven about all of this? This was my own fault. Some wise soul once said that we should be careful what we say, 'for words have wings, and can never be recalled', and Einstein definitely said something about the equation of success being work + play + keeping your mouth shut. It was all very well remembering this now.

My phone vibrated. Betty. I scanned the text message and felt my blood pressure rise.

"Oh God… Abra, listen to this: 'Really soz! Dropped you in it with Nick, accidentally mentioned you came to his last night. He thinks you don't want to see him… ' That's exactly why I told her not to say anything!" I wailed, before continuing to read. "'He said Abra had hinted something was up too. Anyway, oops all round. Soz again x Betty.' I slammed the phone onto the table and looked at Abra, speechless with fury.

"OK," she began carefully, "I know this is all a bit crap, but maybe this is all happening for a reason, perhaps everything's telling you that you need to talk to Nick properly."

"I was going to do that anyway, when the time was right, now things are just that little bit more complicated thanks to you lot." Abra opened her mouth to protest but I held up my hand and continued. "I know you all mean well, but bloody hell… He's had all of this from two angles in one night, plus there's the fact that I didn't want to see him the night before. It's no surprise he thinks I don't want to be with him."

"It does sound a bit like you don't want to be with him."

"I just… there are a few issues and yes, I have been avoiding him recently, mainly because of his stupid weird house, but he doesn't know that. I'm going to have to talk to him now, aren't I? Today."

Abra smiled. "Good luck. I know talking isn't exactly his strong point."

"It's certainly your strong point, and Betty's." I grabbed my bag and threw some cash onto the table.

"What about this bucket of coffee, Sylv? You've still got a good hour's worth of work to do there."

"I'd like to get to Nick's before Pearl phones him up and tells him I've gone off him," I said. "Or Ange sends a carrier pigeon with the message that I don't ever want to see him again, or… "

"Got it," replied Abra, sitting back and finishing her milkshake noisily.

I walked quickly home, jumped straight into my Mini and drove to Nick's, heart pounding. The roads were clogged with Sunday drivers which was fine by me. I didn't feel ready for this conversation, even though it had to happen, and the sooner the better. Finally my wheels crunched into the drive next to the Citroën.

Only 11.50am. Early in Nick-land but I couldn't wait any longer. I dug out my keys, cautiously letting myself in. I called his name. No response. I called again as I walked up to the bedroom. Unmade bed still warm to the touch, mug of tepid coffee. No Nick. Heading back down the ancient, groaning stairs, my bright little car caught my eye through the landing window. It was tempting to run straight back to it and drive away, but no; this needed fixing. I could wait and, if anything happened in the meantime, well, I was going to have to deal with it.

I walked into the kitchen, flicked on the kettle and started up the computer on the worktop, opening up Facebook, in automatic pilot mode. Various updates marched down the page, their inanity briefly numbing my nerves. 'Pearl Gomez is having breakfast in bed.' 'Betty Sinclair is in the dog-house. SAD FACE!' I narrowed my eyes. Yes. Yes, you bloody well are. Abra had posted a picture of her milkshake. A rock star had died. Every grasping also-ran in my timeline was posting about it, somehow managing to make it about themselves. It really was time to deactivate my account for a bit.

My listless scrolling was interrupted by Nick's doorbell. Through the window, I could see a man holding what looked like Nick's Keytar. He caught sight of me and waved. It had to be Sam. Betty was right. He did have a 'nice' face. I felt better as soon as I looked at it.

"You must be Sylvie," he said as he lifted the confounded thing into the hall. "Sam. Is Nick in?"

"I'm waiting for him myself," I said, shaking the hand he'd offered and walking back into the kitchen. "I've made tea if you want one." Sam followed tentatively.

I was relieved to have someone else there, I almost didn't mind who it was. But it helped that it was someone like him. We sat opposite each other at the breakfast bar and smiled nervously, both of us thinking the same thought: if Nick walks in any time soon...

"So, you're getting married, you and Nick?" said Sam, breaking the charged silence.

"Um, yes. Probably next year." I felt a rush of guilt as I tried to ignore the feeling in my stomach and Betty's words ringing in my ears. *Think about Nick*, I urged myself. *That's why you're here.* I was attracted to men who had the shades resolutely drawn, for better or worse. Sam practically radiated positivity. This was a first. I was brought abruptly back to reality by a commotion outside. Brando was being terrorised by next door's tabby.

"You'll have to excuse me. Brando doesn't know how to defend himself against cats, and this one's a bit of a bruiser." I pushed open the stiff patio door and hurried down the garden clapping my hands in a bid to frighten the tubby feline, before scooping up Brando as the cat sauntered proudly away, evidently believing my clapping to be applause. When I came back in, Sam was no longer in the kitchen. He was standing in the hall, his ear pressed to the door of the drawing room. "Shh! I heard something," he whispered.

My heart sank and I held Brando tighter. "What? What did you hear?" Almost before I'd finished my sentence the sound of slow, heavy breathing – almost snoring – drifted from underneath the door. We looked at each other. That's no ghost, I thought. That's Nick.

"I thought you said he wasn't in?" whispered Sam.

"I didn't think he was. It's been totally silent in here. He didn't respond when I called. He always told me this room was locked, that he'd lost the key." I put Brando down and approached the door. "I've heard other stuff from behind this door. Strange stuff. Sounds stupid now, but I'd started to think this place was haunted."

"Doesn't sound that stupid." Sam looked through the keyhole. It was hard to see anything in the semi-darkness. He lay down, peering under the door. A whiff of burnt sweetness hit his nose. "I can see his hand."

"I don't think you need to whisper, Sam. He's out cold." I couldn't believe that after all the farcical ghost-hunting, the sleepless nights, the dread of setting foot in this house, it was Nick all along. I had an awful feeling I knew what was going on, and if it was what I suspected, well, I'd have taken the ghost any day.

"Can you see anything else?"

"Just his arm. I can practically touch it," he said.

"Let me." I lay flat and reached my fingers through the gap. I could just reach Nick's inert hand with my fingertips, and tried to prod it a few times. His arm slowly dragged itself away from the door as he changed position. The bitter-sweet odour made me feel sick.

"Oh no."

I retreated unsteadily, my hands rising to my face. Sam looked under the door to see the huddle of objects that had been obscured by Nick's hand: a blackened spoon, a square of foil, a lighter, the tip of a little needle, a cotton ball, all gathered together like divining bones.

"God," murmured Sam, straightening back up. "You had no idea?"

I shook my head, leaning back on the panelled wall. Something told me Nick probably wouldn't have had to leave the comfort of his own home if he wanted heroin, or anything else for that matter. Dealers would make it as easy as possible for a well-heeled client like Nick; I'd seen how it worked in various capacities around Concierge.

This was the secret I wasn't allowed to be touched by. I felt hurt, not so much that he was using, but that he couldn't let me in on what he was going through, let alone why he was doing it now. Maybe this was pride taking over, but I felt rejected, as if he was choosing someone else over me, someone who knew him better.

"I can't stay here. I have to work out what I'm going to do," I said, almost to myself. "Does anyone else know? I need to get some idea of how blind I've been."

"No one's said anything," insisted Sam, holding out his hands to help me back up. "No disrespect, but everyone in Concierge is pretty self-absorbed. I think even if he was nodding out in front of them they wouldn't think anything of it. He's so quiet and... well, you know better than anyone what he's like." He placed my coat around my shoulders and handed me my bag.

"Apparently not." I locked the front door and walked to the car. Sam took a card from his wallet and handed it to me. "I don't give my number to every woman I meet," he said, smiling slightly. "If you need someone to talk to, or anything, don't hesitate. Any time."

I bit my lip, dropping the card into my bag. "Thanks."

I felt blank and cold as I drove, as if my emotions had been stopped up completely. By 5pm I found myself sitting, upright and rigid, in my living room, still with my coat on. I had no idea how long I'd been there, no memory of the journey home; just the feeling it had taken forever.

I awoke to the metallic din of dustbin-men crashing around outside, shouting, whistling. I'd fallen asleep on the sofa, still in my clothes from the day before. I felt as if I had a hangover, but without the satisfaction of having earned it.

Swinging my legs down onto the floor, my feet made contact with a scattered pile of make-up, loyalty cards, cigarettes... my handbag having fallen off my lap in the night. I groaned, catching sight of Sam's card among the debris. It brought yesterday back into focus. Nick was using. What happened now? What did it mean in terms of us? In terms of anything? What it did mean was that he'd been lying – for how long, I wasn't sure. It also meant I was far from number one in his life. At least now I knew this was just down to what Nick was sticking into his arm, but it had already tainted what we had.

I made for the kitchen, thoughts colliding inside my pounding head. All of my options seemed too black and white. I popped two Anadins out of their blister pack, swallowing them without water.

My phone alerted me to a text from Nick, sent at around midnight. 'My Sylvie.' He's worried, guilty. 'Were you here today? Your Facebook page was open. Sorry I was out. Come over tomorrow.' More lies. Stepping over the contents of my handbag, I picked up Sam's card and looked at it again. Just the sight of it made me feel better. We were practically strangers but he'd already become my closest ally. And he did say, "Call anytime"… but no, I couldn't. It was too early, I told myself, keying in his number and saving it all the same.

The only person I could realistically talk to at this stage was Betty, although how she would take the news that her brother was on heroin, I didn't know. It was now 8am. She would be in the middle of her morning meditation and wouldn't thank me for interrupting, but these were extenuating circumstances.

Without giving myself any more time to think, I called Betty's number. Voicemail. This was too important to wait. I stuffed everything back into my bag and made for the car. The sight of my own street at this time of the morning threw me. It was so busy: stony-faced people in suits and trainers marching towards the bus-stop; 'yummy-mummies' bustling out of houses with neat-looking children in tow; a dog-walker striding towards the park with five hounds of different sizes and colours pulling ahead, tails swishing in the sharp morning air. Everyone seemed so remote from each other.

I glanced in the mirror – eyes ringed with smudged mascara, brown hair still messily resembling an approximation of yesterday's ponytail. I didn't care. It wasn't like Sam was going to be there. And then I caught myself. Sam? I meant Nick, obviously. Yes, Nick. Nick Nick Nick.

By the time I parked up outside Betty's cottage, nestled prettily by the Thames, it was just after 9am. The journey was normally brief but the West London school run, all glossy 4X4s and highlights, put paid to that. At least 9am wasn't unreasonably early to drop in on someone, although that did depend on the someone. If Nick had heard his doorbell ringing at 9am he'd either call the police or assume it was the police. Apart from his sister – and even she was on shaky ground here – he didn't associate with people who woke up at that sort of time, and was suspicious of anyone who did, as was I. But this was Betty. It was safe to knock.

Or so I thought. As I waited for her to answer, muffled shouts, shrieks of laughter and whipping sounds floated down from the upstairs window. Finally Betty came to the door, a waft of incense escaping as it opened.

"Sylvie! You look dreadful! God, what's going on?" said Betty, hauling me inside.

"I might ask you the same thing," I said, nodding towards the stairs as I sat down in the fragrant kitchen.

"What do you mean?" she said hesitantly. At that moment there was a crash and a yell from upstairs, accompanied by more hoots of female laughter. Betty winked at me. Heavy footsteps thundered down the stairs, practically tripping over themselves in their attempt to get away. It was Johnson Large, or at least I thought it was. I just caught a glimpse of a large man wearing very little hurtling past the kitchen door. Moments later, the brief silence was ripped apart by the sound of a powerful motorbike haring off.

"So… " I said, turning back to Betty.

"It's Gomez and his harem," she muttered, rolling her eyes. "They stayed over because they're having their bedroom redone. More mirrors. I mean, mirrors everywhere. Some of them are magnifying ones – Gomez's idea. And," Betty paused for dramatic effect, "they are installing a marble sculpture of an absolutely huge… "

"Just get to the point."

Betty dunked a biscuit into her coffee, swishing it back and forth. "Gomez wanted his back, sack and crack waxing, so Ange and Pearl have been busy doing that. Gomez texted Johnson because he knew *he* was due for a B S and C, so that's why he was here. Anyway, one thing led to another, as it always does. Then they found my old riding crop from when I used to ride in the New Forest. Anyway, they… like that sort of thing, Pearl and Gomez. They started messing around with that and I don't know, I suppose it all went too far for Johnson. I don't know if I'll be getting that crop back any time soon. "

"You might not want it back. And isn't it a bit early in the day for those kind of … shenanigans?"

"It's their age," concluded Betty. "Anyway, what's going on? You look like a zombie. You haven't even brushed your hair. Or your eyebrows. Things must be serious."

"My… eyebrows?" I touched them self-consciously. They didn't feel especially out of control.

"You look like Denis Healy," confirmed Betty. "Now what is it? Ghost action?" I had to disappoint her. Seriously disappoint her.

I hugged myself and leant over my coffee, allowing the steam to warm my nose. Once again I'd gone in without thinking about how I was going to discuss a very delicate subject. Betty was waiting, her blue-rimmed eyes fixed on me like a lemur. I stalled by pouring a trickle of milk slowly into my coffee, watching it rise back to the surface like sand-clouds.

"There is no ghost," I said. "It's Nick."

"The noises?"

"All Nick."

"But you said he was always out," protested Betty. The last vestiges of belief in her brother were dissolving.

"I went there yesterday, Sam was there too – Nick was asleep in that room, practically comatose. We could hear him breathing. I looked under the door and… God, I don't know how to tell you this."

"I knew it." I looked up at Betty. Her normally glowing face was turning grey. I didn't know whether the woman in front of me was going to shrink into despair or turn to steel, taking care of the situation like a sergeant major.

"I *knew* it," she repeated, wiping down surfaces, refilling the kettle, mindless displacement activities. "I saw the signs. Or maybe I've been trying not to. I'm sorry, darling, but you need to know this is not the first time for Nick." She stopped and leant heavily on the worktop. I felt my temperature plunge. It made complete sense, but the fact everyone felt they had to keep his past a secret from me was more upsetting than the fact this had happened before. I hated that he'd had to keep all of this inside, away from me, for fear of … what? Me leaving? If I'd have been more aware, maybe I'd have been able to stop this from happening. I couldn't speak. But what I was feeling couldn't have compared with what Betty was going through right now.

"I saw it in his eyes the other night," she continued dully. "It was all so familiar. I even asked him outright."

"Just like that?"

"At least it makes sense of those bloody noises."

I rewound the recent past, trying to zone in on whether he'd been displaying signs of heroin use. The problems had started once the tour was over, correlating perfectly with his legendary period of adjustment. He was sweating more at night, he was more switched-off. When I thought about it, I rarely saw him eat. I rarely saw him at all.

"What are you going to do, Sylvie?"

"Help him?"

"Easier said than done. And not pretty," said Betty, sitting back down with a refilled mug. It was a mug of cold water. Betty had forgotten to switch on the kettle, let alone add any coffee. She was oblivious, in shock, but her outward air of control was galvanising by the second.

"It took a long time for him to give up the first time," she said. "He's older now, it's going to be harder. It took long enough for him to decide he even wanted to give up. That's the problem with drugs, they are actually quite enjoyable."

"I'll be there for him, whatever he chooses to do."

"See previous answer," said Betty.

"Well, I'm marrying him!"

Betty smiled. "Nick is my brother and I love him. But you're family to me now too, and believe me, I wouldn't want any of my loved ones to marry a… well, a junkie. He will lie, his capacity for love is diminishing, soon you'll barely recognise him. He'll only be capable of caring about one thing." Betty continued psychobabbling, as if the words were being regurgitated from memory, originally delivered by a well-paid therapist and stored up from the last time, emerging from beneath layers of other experiences and newer memories, readily accessed when required. She briefly became aware of me again. "It's not personal."

I didn't know what I'd expected Betty to say, but I didn't think it would be this. I'd thought Betty might break down, freak out... this was just brutal. It was the truth, basically, pouring out of her mouth, building a dark picture of our future. Betty broke off when she noticed my face.

"What I'm saying is, to paraphrase Lady Di, there'll be three of you in that marriage if he stays on smack. Obviously she didn't say the 'smack' bit, but same principle. It doesn't matter what vows you take. You'll just never be as important."

A knock at the door made us both jump, and I sat, motionless, staring into my cup as Betty rose to answer it. The voice at the door, which could just about be heard in between Betty's gushing and the racket upstairs, was Sam's. Great. I had possibly never looked worse. Well, maybe once, in that school photo with the braces, but not in my adult life. Well... perhaps in my most recent passport photo but that didn't count. No one looked good in those. There was one solution: as immature as it made me feel, I was going to have to hide – although there didn't seem to be anywhere I could go, no utility room, no back door. Like an eight-year-old, I slunk under the table and felt royally idiotic while I was at it, by the way.

"Gaffer tape?" asked Betty, twirling the black roll around her finger.

"Yep. Gomez texted, he said he needed it urgently," replied Sam. "He told me he'd be here, and I wasn't far away so... "

"Ah right," said Betty. "I'll make sure he gets it." There was a crash of several people falling off a bed followed by gales of hilarity.

"Everything OK?"

"Yes! Now, I'd invite you in but I need to get on, and of course, Gomez needs his gaffer tape. I think he's... erm... "

"He said he was fixing a mic-stand?" offered Sam. He knew that was a lie. Gomez didn't even fix his own hair. The idea was as likely as Nick announcing he was leaving Concierge to become a children's entertainer. It was part of Sam's job not to ask questions.

"Exactly," said Betty. "Fixing a mic-stand. Sylvie is here if you want to say hello." Damn you, Betty.

I made sure I was obscured by a conveniently positioned flap of tablecloth. Through the lacy material I watched two pairs of feet approaching, one in sparkly cream sandals, one in blue Converse boots. I held my breath.

"Well, she was here."

"She isn't... upstairs, is she?"

Betty shook her head. "Doubt it." And then she spotted me, catching my eye as I glared up at her through the holes in the lace. Incredibly, she resisted the urge to blow my cover. "Well, if that's everything?" She ushered him back out and I exhaled.

I crawled out, wriggling my foot madly to break up the cramp that was taking hold. "No need to explain," said Betty, poking her head around the kitchen door. "I wouldn't want to be seen by someone I fancied if I wasn't looking my best." Before I had time to protest, she was rushing up the stairs. I heard various cries of "Aha!" and the sound of tape being unwound tore through the air. Betty shut the door and glided back down to the kitchen.

"Gaffer tape, eh?"

"Doesn't matter," replied Betty brusquely, shutting the door. She sat back down at the table, and paused, rolling a biscuit crumb under her finger. "So, Sam... Ha! First bit of colour I've seen in your face since you've been here." It almost didn't matter what I said now, a blush was a blush, and I could feel it spreading until it felt as if even my hair had gone pink.

"You like him. I'm not surprised."

"Betty… "

"I know, I know, you love Nick, Nick loves you, but I can see the bigger picture." She smoothed my bird's-nest hair and looked at me. "Sylvie, I'd love – *love* – to be able to call you my sister-in-law but I also want you to be happy. You do have a choice. Even if there was no one else in the picture… "

"There is no one else in the picture."

"Yes, well… Even if there *was* no one else in the picture, you don't have to stay in this situation. I've seen so many women waste any chances of happiness waiting for a partner who will never give up an addiction. If it was me, Sylvie, I would be out of there."

"I don't know. Things have been difficult, and there's a… situation that makes me feel uncomfortable."

"And might not go away."

"Yes, all right, and might not go away. But I can't just start acting as if I've already moved on. I need to think about this."

"Think about it by all means. I know what happens."

"What do you mean, you know what happens? We're not talking about renting a film. What makes you think it's going to be the same as before?"

"I mean," said Betty gently, "I read the cards when you and Nick got engaged. The tarot cards, I mean, not the engagement cards. Although I read them too; some lovely messages… But anyway, the tarot cards – Sylvie, that deck has never let me down. Everything is going to be OK, more than OK, in fact. It's just the longer you take to decide… well, what you want to do, the longer you put off what could be just right."

I couldn't believe what I was hearing. The last couple of days had been so overwhelming I couldn't deal with the idea that Betty was now convinced she could see my future because of some cards she'd laid out, probably while drunk. "I have to go," I breathed, getting up and pulling my coat on. "I need a proper sleep, this is all a bit much." Betty accompanied me to the door.

"They've gone very quiet up there," I added.

Don't worry about them, I'll make sure they haven't killed each other. Go home, get some rest, have something to eat. Just don't forget we've got that charity gig tomorrow at the Roundhouse. We need to be there by 3pm."

"God, of course." I had indeed forgotten about it. The list of everything I had to do rushed towards me. Cleaning, steaming, sorting, hanging... Nick alone had three costume-changes. There was, of course, the distinct possibility that he wouldn't even turn up. This would be the acid test. In a way I wanted him to let us down – I wanted him to have to face himself. I also knew it would be hard to take if he could get himself together for a gig, but not for me.

Saturday, 3.45pm. The boom of the Concierge sound-check shook the walls of the Roundhouse and floated into the backstage car park, an area peopled entirely of smoking roadies, technicians and early-bird autograph-hunters. I was late. I'd overslept.

Stressed out and almost entirely obscured by an armful of clothes, I pushed my way through to the dressing rooms. Gomez and his ladies had already commandeered Dressing Room One, I gathered from the noises behind the door. I could hear a mopey adolescent voice droning away below the chatter of Pearl and Ange and Gomez's familiar rasp, and this meant that Aduki, Gomez's perpetually embarassed teenage son, was also here. Once upon a time I'd have been expected to keep Gomez's scowling offspring entertained while everyone else partied. Fortunately he could look after himself now, which was just as well, because, even though I could appreciate he hadn't had the most regular upbringing, I still found him to be a miserable scrote.

Johnson had dumped his stuff in Dressing Room Two, and was walking rather carefully into the corridor as I approached. He had a look of indignation etched on his booze-aged face, and as I smiled and brushed past he jerked back defensively. Whatever Pearl and co. had done yesterday at Betty's had evidently left him traumatised. Abra was in Dressing Room Three, spraying her Afro with something industrial.

"Afternoon," I said, dropping the clothes on a chair and approaching for a hug.

"Woah there. You're not supposed to get too close to this stuff."

"Says the person spraying it on her head," I said.

"It's Flame-Retard. And I'm spraying it on my wig – big difference." It was true, the wig was so voluminous that it stood about a foot away from her head. Her scalp would be safe.

"Don't tell me they're using pyrotechnics tonight," I sighed.

Abra swung round and looked at me. "No pyrotechnics. Not planned ones anyway. It's Henson Bedges. Didn't Nick tell you all this? He's back and Les is worried he's going to try to set fire to everyone. Or me at least." She started spritzing her catsuit.

"Is Henson Bedges the one… "

'Who sets fire to things? Yep. Les reckons he's out for blood, or at least his old job. Which is a bit crazy because I thought he was dead. That's showbiz." She gave the pile of Nick's clothes a quick spray. "Any more supernatural experiences? I hear the ghost-hunting didn't bear any fruit."

"Turns out it's not a ghost," I said, feeling like a fool for having even thought it.

"Well, that's a relief," said Abra, turning back to her mirror and admiring herself.

Dressing Room Four was empty except for a chair, a kettle and a set-list. There was no evidence of Nick. I tried to keep my mind clear, checking myself in the full-length mirror. I brushed down my dress before hanging up Nick's clothes – all of them black – as Les's booming voice approached.

"Got that? Ginger hair, smells awful. Do not under any circumstances let him in. And don't forget to put Tony Hadley plus five on the door," he shouted to the stage door before striding in. "Where's Laughing Boy?"

"I don't know, Les, I'm not his keeper." I fiddled with the costumes on the hangers, refusing to meet his eye. It was par for the course for the first question in any conversation to concern my significant other – a phenomenon endured by the rest of the Coven and partners of pop stars the world over. It was never "How are you?" It was always "How's the fella? What's he up to? Where is he?" Even Abra got it from over-eager fans who assumed she must be having a relationship with a band-member to have got the gig. It was a mistake they would only make once, granted. OK, Les couldn't be blamed for asking, but I was even more sensitive about it now.

"Whatever, I need him here ASAP." (Les always pronounced this as 'ay-sap'.) "We sound-checked without him, we can't do the bleeding gig without him. And there's a meeting in twenty minutes in the production office. I need him there."

Gomez poked his angry face around the door. "Les?!"

"What?"

"What do you think? Poxy rider, is what." Gomez was holding a plastic packet between his fingertips in a disdainful manner. "This sandwich is not working for me."

"Lucky fucking sandwich," growled Les, rubbing his head as he always did in times of turmoil. He walked back out, Gomez scuttling after him. "FIND NICK," Les bellowed over his shoulder as he disappeared down the corridor.

"I'm not his keeper," I repeated, accidentally pulling a metal spike off the shoulder of a Yohji Yamamoto jacket. After a couple of attempts to reattach it, I shoved it into my pocket and fell back onto the threadbare sofa. It smelt of ganja and biscuits. I remembered when I first started working with bands, my friends were convinced I was living a life of glamour. I wouldn't have changed it for the world, but glamour was not a word that sprang to mind right now.

Then I thought about those friends, people I'd not seen in nearly three years. After the twentieth time you turn down a party, a hen-night, even a wedding because they always fall on the nights you are working, you just lose touch. Now my life revolved firmly around the band. It had sucked me in completely. It was like living in a parallel universe, which could be a good thing at times. If I was honest, I didn't really want to live in the real world. I'd certainly picked the right band for that.

"Hullo." Sam was hovering by the door. Seeing him elicited so many mixed feelings. I immediately associated his friendly, open face with that horrible afternoon at Nick's house, but I was pleased to see him. More pleased than I should have been.

"Come in." I got up. "Coffee?" Thank God for the kettle, I thought. Such a leveller. Such a great social prop.

"Working hard, eh?"

I smiled at his reflection in the mirror as I shook granules into cups. "I know how it might have looked."

"Don't tell me you were meditating as well. I couldn't get Gomez to sound-check before he'd done 108 mantras. Wouldn't budge. Practically bit my head off once he'd finished too. I thought meditation was supposed to encourage serenity."

"Imagine what he'd be like if he didn't do it," I said, willing the kettle to boil faster. Someone at the sound desk was playing Led Zeppelin's 'Communication Breakdown' through the PA, Robert Plant's screams charging through every doorway, under every crack, every chord so familiar they were like old friends, earthing me. The fact I was feeling so fluttery was bad. Sam sat on the arm of the sofa.

"Listen, I'd wanted to check you were OK after— "

"ARGH CHRIST," I screamed, running to the sink. "Burnt my fucking hand!"

Sam sprang into action, splashing my stinging red hand with cold water. This was an opportunity for him to go into Knight in Shining Armour mode. Again. He was getting pretty good at it. Once the drama had subsided, we sat together, me staring sadly at my sore, glowing fingers.

"Is there anything I can do?"

"I've got some aloe vera in my bag, that should help," I said, about to get up. Sam pushed me back down and rooted through the bag himself, determined to assist.

"This it?" He held up a bottle of perfume.

"No. Smaller. Green with a gold label."

"This?"

"No, that's sun-screen. Let me... "

"No! I'm helping. This?"

"That's the one. I'll take it from here." But Sam insisted on squeezing way too much onto my hand and massaging it in vigorously. I flinched a little. "Bit gentler please, Matron."

"Sorry," he said. "I'm making it worse." He leant down, lifted my hand and kissed it, before resuming Mission Injured Paw, more softly this time, bantering to nullify the intimacy. I continued to stare hard at my hand where it had been kissed, too nervous to look at his face. Sam refused to look up too, but we had an excuse to touch and exist just briefly in the bubble of warmth we'd created on that unlovely sofa. The tops of our heads were almost touching. I felt he was genuine, but I also felt we had to break away from one another, and do it soon. Anyone walking in right now – anyone but Betty – would naturally assume Sam was steaming in on me, taking advantage of my fragile situation with Nick.

Who, incidentally, was standing in the doorway, and had been for some time.

Sam and I looked up dumbly as seconds passed in excruciating silence. For one unhinged moment I wondered whether I might later be able to convince Nick that this had all been a drug-induced dream, but he seemed irritatingly lucid. He reached into his pocket and took out a cigarette.

"Um... there's a £500 fine for smoking in the building, Nick," said Sam, gesturing at a sign on the wall.

"Make it a grand," Nick replied coldly. "I'll be having another in half an hour." He continued to stare. Suddenly aware of myself, I extricated my hand from Sam's.

"I... burnt my hand, Sam was just... "

"Kissing it. Yeah, I saw."

"How long have you been there?" said Sam, incredulous. I elbowed him in the stomach and he rose, mumbling something about amplifiers, and attempted to slink past Nick without having to touch him. Nick eventually sloped away from the door and took a beer from the fridge. His face remained inscrutable.

"You've been very elusive." That was all he said. Didn't even say any more about the fact he'd watched his future wife getting cosy with another man. I supposed that was the ultimate insult to a rival alpha male, not even considering his attentions worthy of concern. This was worse than if he'd wanted to talk about it;

I just wanted to be told off and have done with it. But no, I was having to face the raw wound that was us by a more direct route, avoiding the Sam detour and heading straight down into a Nick-shaped dead end. The irony was not lost on me that I was the one considering how to broach this subject and now, as if by really annoying magic, Nick had gone and broached it himself when I was at my least prepared.

"Elusive. That's interesting coming from you." I was quaking from the inside out. Nerves, rage, it was all there. And then I did it. I blurted it out. Despite myself.

"I know, you know."

"I know you know," responded Nick in his trademark monotone, leaning his head on his hand.

"That's what I just said. God." I knew drugs could arrest mental maturity (or so I'd read online – wedding research had taken a back seat for websites about heroin abuse), but if he was just going to repeat everything I said back to me, he was more 'arrested' than I thought. I had a flash of my possible future as a cross between a mother and a carer. To a grown man. A casualty. I didn't like it. No, I did not.

"I mean, I know that you know. About my sickness."

"You're not sick," I spat, tingling with fury. Fury at Nick, fury at Betty for going over my head and telling him. But particularly Nick. "People with cancer are sick. You chose to do this." I was being unreasonable but fuck it. I was in no mood for his victim complex. It wasn't all about him.

"Whatever you want to call it," said Nick, picking at the label on his beer. "'Problem'. I understand why you couldn't talk to me but— "

"Why couldn't you talk to *me*? You just lied. All those times you said you were out... What the hell has driven you back to this?"

"And now," Nick talked over me. "You're slipping away from me."

"*I'm* slipping away?"

"Towards someone else. Makes sense. You don't want to be with an addict."

"A liar, I don't want to be with a liar," I corrected. "The whole point of marriage is that you don't have to be on your own. We're not even married yet and I'm lonely; you are too, you must be. But you're cutting yourself off, you're not even giving me the chance to support you." The words flew out of my mouth in a volley, crashing against him and shattering into shards. "You think you're the only one affected by this. Maybe you thought you were protecting me by— "

"NICK!" Les barked from the other side of the door, his voice edged with hysteria. "I need you and Sylvie in the production office."

I blinked slowly against the intrusion. "We'll talk later."

"At my place?"

"No, mine." I was tired of everything being on Nick's terms, tired of even thinking about that house. We could make new memories there when he was clean. In the meantime...

"NOW," yelled Les from further down the corridor. Nick pulled himself to his feet and we left the room, an icy yard of space between us.

*

The production office was heaving, band, crew and entourage squeezed into every available space, a riot of ludicrous outfits, man-scara and teased hair. Les was sitting behind a desk, arms folded. The room was quiet but for the impatient tapping of his brogue on the floor.

I scanned the room but couldn't see Sam. Betty avoided my gaze. I glared at her anyway. Then there was a tug on my sleeve. Sam was right next to me. Sandwiched in a confined space between Nick and Sam. How humorous the Universe was feeling today.

"Right," said Les. "You all know about the situation with Henson Bedges. Abra will be passing around Flame-Retard spray for use on costumes and other combustibles." Abra dutifully waggled the can in the air.

"Now, I wouldn't normally make this kind of address before a show, as I know how sensitive some of you can be. " He looked at Gomez before continuing. "But unfortunately, I've had to raise the Bedges risk factor to high alert." A murmur of consternation rippled through the room. Abra's confident expression evaporated.

"I've received another missive," continued Les darkly. "It was hand-delivered to the stage door less than an hour ago." He took a large envelope from the inside of his Crombie. All eyes were on Les, who was secretly loving the attention. He shook the contents of the envelope onto the table: four loose burnt matches and a coffee-stained publicity shot of Henson from Concierge's heyday. Les held up the picture to the room solemnly. But the picture, which at first glance just appeared to be an image of a huge explosion of ginger hair, was nothing. What was on the back was even more disturbing.

"£1000 OR YOU BURN TONIGHT", spelled out in glued-on charred matches. Actually it was spelt "Or you bun tonight". Presumably the four loose matches were meant to be the 'R' but had made a break for it. Bedges was nothing if not creative, and relatively adept at handicrafts to boot. Give him a more reliable adhesive and who knows what he could achieve.

"A grand?" chuckled Gomez. "You'd think he'd ask for a bit more than that."

"He's probably owed ten times that in unclaimed royalties," said Les. "He'd make more money if he just sorted his accounts out. There's more to this than meets the eye."

Underneath the message were typed instructions (he'd tired of the matches) of where and when the money should be delivered. At 7.30pm, an hour before they were due to go on, Gomez – it had to be Gomez – was required to meet Bedges in the car park with the cash. Alone.

"Me? He'll... he'll kill me!" half-screamed Gomez.

"Can't we just call the police?" I interjected.

Les looked at me. "I'd prefer not to get the police involved." Gomez made a struggling attempt to get out of the room but failed, being as he was wedged into the corner furthest from the door. His options for theatricality were limited. He considered falling dramatically to his knees, but then realised no one would be able to see past the many bodies already semi-obscuring him. He settled on thumping his fist tragically on the wall.

"Why no police?" I persisted.

"The last time we called the police on Bedges, he got out of it, made out there was some mistake, said the air stewardess had set light to her own hair, all that bollocks. The police were star-struck and he was let off. But after that, he got worse. He felt betrayed and now he's even more barmy – if I call the police this time, lives could be at stake.

"Now," he continued. "Something tells me once we've handed that money over it won't be the end of it. It's too small an amount and I don't trust Bedges. Security will be tight, but all the same I've decided, for damage limitation purposes, that for tonight's show you will all be wearing helmets."

"All of us?" asked Pearl, self-consciously touching her hair.

"Just the band," sighed Les. "Obviously. In case of incendiary missiles."

"Helmets. Of course. Never mind the fact I've just had a mother-fucking BLOW-DRY," shrieked Gomez. "Will this absolute SHITE of a day never END?"

"Beam me up, Scotty," said Nick under his breath.

Les, wild-eyed, yanked a handkerchief from his top pocket and wiped his streaming forehead. "I think that's everything," he said shakily, producing another envelope and handing it to Pearl. "The money – 7.30pm, in the car park, OK Gomez? You've got two hours to go hysterical in the meantime. Now get out, all of you. I can hardly breathe. Sylvie, the helmets will be at the stage door."

Les briefly shuffled some papers in front of him like a newsreader before pretending to write. Room dismissed.

The helmets, which had indeed arrived at stage door, were all different, owing to the fact that this was a last-minute development. I knocked discreetly on Johnson's door and placed a motorcycle helmet outside, dropped off a roomier horned Viking helmet (better for singing) for Gomez, gave a little Roman number to Abra who was glumly removing her wig, and chose a Knights' Templar affair for Nick. I thought he'd appreciate that more than the Dad's Army-style tin hat that had been included in the order as a spare. I considered hanging on to that for myself. My head was spinning. Part of me was quite grateful for the arrival of another drama to shunt my own situation off top-billing, but it was all just prolonging the inevitable.

Minutes ticked by, the susurrus of early punters arriving front of house trickling through the dressing room tannoys. Somehow, amid the tension, noise and unresolved pre-marital issues, Nick had managed to fall into a deep sleep, his long frame crumpled on the sofa like a dead spider. Gomez and his harem could be heard chanting feverishly from their dressing room, the droning punctuated occasionally by the solemn clang of a Tibetan cymbal. Johnson's door was firmly locked (although the helmet had been snatched inside) and Abra was already wearing her Roman helmet and little else, and was rapidly thrumming the strings of her bass. Her door, conversely, was wide open.

I wandered the backstage area, breathing in the hairspray and Flame-Retard, marijuana and spilt beer, taking in those pre-gig moments when everything is ready and there's nothing to do but wait. But tonight that anticipation wasn't just about the show. This was the calm before the storm.

At 7.25pm, Gomez walked silently up the corridor towards Les at the stage door. Everyone gawked after him from various doorways. Les glared and the heads simultaneously receded. I climbed onto the table and peered out of the window into the car park, spotting squares of light from the dressing room windows reflected in the shiny black tour bus parked a few metres away. Within those illuminated boxes were familiar silhouettes, rubber-necking from their own vantage points.

Sure enough, at the promised time, a motorcycle and sidecar purred into view and a tall leather-clad figure dismounted, locks of carroty hair poking out from underneath the motorcycle helmet. It was Bedges, twitching with agitation, waiting for Gomez to come closer. I couldn't help observing that this Bedges had a large behind for a bloke. Must have been all those years sitting and obsessing over revenge. Brooding is probably a fairly sedentary occupation.

"What you doing up there?" slurred Nick, coming round from his coma. As I turned to explain, there was a shout and sounds of a scuffle, followed by a primal scream from Pearl two rooms up. Bedges and Gomez were locked in combat, which was soon over when Bedges played dirty and kneed him in the groin before practically stuffing him into the sidecar. By the time Les, Pearl,

Ange and Johnson had rushed into the car park, the pair had roared off, Bedges holding two fingers aloft as he sped away.

"Holy crap."

"What's with all the screaming?"

"Gomez is being kidnapped."

"Oh."

"Nick, I'm serious." I watched Les trying to make a call as Pearl and Ange wailed and thumped him from both sides. By the time Nick and I had headed into the car park ourselves, the rest of the entourage had already filed out, unsure of what to say or do. Aduki was in a state of silent shock, although it was hard for the untrained eye to spot the difference between that and his usual demeanour. I sometimes wondered whether he wasn't Nick's son rather than Gomez's. I chose not to ponder this too often.

"Tell me that was the police," I said to Les as the delirium died down. Les nodded sternly. "Said they'd be here ay-sap. In the meantime, we need to work out how we're going to do this fucking gig. Stage-time is in one hour."

"You're not suggesting we go on after that?" said Johnson. "It's... it's disrespectful."

"And impossible," added Nick. "None of us can sing."

"Never stopped Gomez," said Abra.

"Aduki!" roared Les, swinging round to face the youth. "Can ya sing?" he said, trying to sound jovial. "The fans would love it if Gomez's son was on stage. You'll be the hero of the night." Aduki appeared to shrink several inches.

"You can't be serious," said Ange. "He just watched his own father getting kidnapped."

"Why don't *you* do it?" said Betty, approaching Les with her hands on her hips. "In the movie business, a director should never tell an actor to do anything they wouldn't be prepared to do themselves. Anyway, I've heard you sing, and you're very good." Betty prodded him twice on the chest as she said the last two words of her sentence.

"Ridiculous," said Les, buttoning his Crombie in order to shield himself from any more prods. "Besides, when have you heard me sing?"

"At my New Year's party. You gave a passable 'Auld Lang Syne'."

"I liked his version of 'Yesterday Once More' during the last after-show," added Ange.

"For goodness' sake, this is serious," Les huffed, walking away from Betty.

Johnson barred his path. "You'll be wearing a helmet. No one will know it's you."

"You are all being very silly," said Les, his colour rising.

"We'll have to cancel the gig then," shrugged Nick. "Shame. All those people out there... and it's for charity. You'll have to tell them, Les."

"Shut up, Nick," Les growled, trying not to imagine the colourful reaction of 1700 Concierge fans being told the gig was off.

"Les, just try the Viking helmet," pleaded Abra.

"NO," bellowed Les. "NO, NO, NO, NO, NO."

*

"Bastards," said Les from underneath the echoing helmet as Sam checked the mouth-piece attached to his face. "Absolute... total... bastards. All of you. I've never hated you more."

"You are doing us – and all of those people out there – a huge favour," soothed Johnson, patting him on the head, his rings clanging against the metal.

"DON'T," yelled Les. "It's like being inside fucking Big Ben."

"Sorry."

"What about the police?"

"We'll take care of it," said Betty. "Just do your stuff." She guided him into the wings. Fortunately he could only see the floor and not the crowd of expectant faces.

"Wait," said Les, his hands searching to grab whoever was near. "The songs. I don't know if I can remember them all. Oh God, this is like one of those anxiety dreams."

"Surely you remember a few. You've been working with us for the past twenty-five years," said Johnson.

"Doesn't mean I've been listening."

"We can throw in 'Auld Lang Syne' and 'Yesterday Once More' if you get desperate," said Nick. He was joking, but sure enough, four numbers in and Concierge found themselves 'sha-la-la-la-ing' and 'shooby-doo-lang-langing' uncertainly in front of a livid sea of fans. The pint-throwing had begun and Les even received a glancing blow on the head with a Zippo halfway through his destruction of the Carpenters' hit. He struggled on but people were soon hurling anything they could get their hands on.

Valiantly Les continued until a furious fan defied security, mounted the stage, whipped off Les's helmet and punched him in the face before holding a triumphant fist aloft before the baying audience. Les responded by attempting to strangle his attacker, but more fuming men in Concierge T-shirts were clambering up. The rest of the band downed tools and ran for cover while Sam and another two roadies dragged Les out of the fray, leaving the venue's security officers to sort out the mess.

An announcement went over the tannoy from a shaky-voiced front of house manager explaining that Gomez was 'indisposed' and that dissatisfied punters could get their money back. Les groaned, reclining on the sofa as Betty dabbed his eye with a wet cotton-pad.

"I'm going to kill each and every one of you for this," Les muttered. "And then, I shall revive you and kill you all again."

"You did what you had to do," said Johnson. "We're all so proud of you."

"Don't start any long books, mate, I mean it."

Ange popped her head around the door. "Coppers want you." Les sat up and pushed Betty away. "Pearl and Aduki have gone home, they're in a right state."

"What time did the police arrive?"

"About half an hour ago. Incidentally, they've cordoned off the back-stage car park. It was getting pretty heavy out there."

"What a night." Les struggled to his feet and clumped out of the dressing room. The police were in the production office, waiting. Everyone scuttled after him to eavesdrop but Les slammed the door. When he emerged he looked even more disconsolate than he did when he went in.

"Henson Bedges, my friends, is dead."

"The police killed him?"

"Course not. He's been dead for years. Police spoke to his widow earlier."

"He was *married*?" said Betty.

"Yes, and for the past decade or so he was a completely reformed character. Moved to California, became a hippy… "

"This is crazy, Les, we saw him," protested Abra.

"You saw someone with red hair. You didn't see his face."

"That's assuming it's even a 'he'," I said. "You have to admit he had quite a womanly behind. And the cut of the leathers, particularly the top-half, were a bit feminine. I think they even had darts."

"Explain," said Les impatiently.

"Little folds that are sewn in around the bustline in women's tops."

"How the hell could you see that?"

"I *think* I saw it. And that hair could have been fake. The texture didn't look like real hair at all. It was like a cheap party wig."

"Well, so was Bedges' barnet, to be fair. But he did look like he'd developed moobs, come to think of it," said Johnson.

Les shook his head and sighed. "Fucking Ada. I can't think of any woman who would go to these kinds of lengths to put the wind up us and kidnap Gomez. I mean, who in their right mind would… Ah. Oh shit."

Ange gave a harsh little intake of breath. "Carly?"

"Who else?" breathed Les. "I thought she'd gone quiet. She used to ring all the time, checking up on Gomez, turning up at gigs, being… mad. It was a nightmare. Then it stopped. I thought she'd got over him, but she was planning this."

It was a long night. Everyone had to go to the police station once it was deemed safe to leave the venue (angry mob or nay, most of the fans were still at the mercy of the last Tube) and the police interviews were endless. Everyone felt wretched by the time we were allowed to leave – particularly Nick. He was breathless, sweating. I noticed him suffering as he leant against his car, and I placed my hand over his heart. It was thudding madly, as if it wanted to jump out of his chest.

"So," I said, retreating to my own car. "You'll be driving to mine now then?" *If you don't have a coronary on the way, natch.*

"Yeah. See you there."

Driving through London in all its shiny-dirty Saturday night glory, I kept checking my rear view mirror to see if Nick's car was behind me. Finally we were going to talk. I was aching for sleep but no, we had to talk first. Sleep was not on the agenda tonight.

We'd only driven as far as Swiss Cottage when Nick veered off to the left. My phone beeped less than a minute later. "Taking a detour, need to get my cigs, see you at yours X." I swerved round to follow him.

Several cars were now between us, all the better for doing some surreptitious Nick-tracking. My eyes were blurred with fatigue but I kept them trained on the target, which soon turned left into a badly-lit residential street. The Citroën pulled up outside a dilapidated house, purple velvet pinned up at filthy windows.

I parked on the corner, hidden from view, and locked my doors, watching Nick's spindly legs rush up the sagging front steps. I'd never seen him rush anywhere. The door opened and he was instantly absorbed into the thick darkness of the house. I watched avidly until my eyes played tricks on me.

The crash and clatter of street-cleaners woke me. It felt as if only a few moments had passed. I checked my phone. Sunday, 5.23am. No word from Nick. I looked at the house that had swallowed my fiancé. His car was still outside. I was half-tempted to get out and knock on the door, but a new feeling took over – that this was none of my business. I didn't want it ever to be any of my business. Stepping over that threshold, seeing Nick in the state I knew he'd be in, would mean stepping into a world I never wanted to experience, even second-hand.

This was the night we were supposed to be sorting things out, and he'd already slunk behind his sad little comfort blanket. I scrabbled in the glove compartment for my sunglasses, pushed them onto my face, and drove.

For some reason a tiny, naïve part of my brain was sure Nick would still come eventually. The rest of my brain was just begging for sleep. I sat at my kitchen table, smoking, drinking coffee and waiting. My head was starting to nod dangerously towards the ashtray when I was jolted awake by a knock at the front door. Betty.

"I'm sorry!" she said, before even saying 'hello'. "I know you're angry with me but I was talking to Nick and it all just came out."

I shook my head and waved her in. "Did us a favour. We inched towards talking about it."

Betty strode to the kitchen and started opening cupboards. "Hold that thought. Where's your Lea and Perrins? God, do you *have* any food?" I was so used to eating out on tour, I still hadn't got into the habit of doing a proper food shop. It was all as-and-when. And Worcestershire Sauce was never high on the list, oddly enough.

"Might be some at the back. I was going to offer coffee."

"Eggs?" Betty had located a fudgy old bottle of brown sauce instead and was now rooting through the fridge.

"You're not pregnant, are you?"

"The issue of my advanced years aside, I believe you have to have sex to get pregnant." Betty rapidly whisked the ingredients together in a cup, a spray of brown droplets spattering the worktop.

"Prairie Oyster? Won't be the same with brown sauce but it should have the same effect, I suppose."

Prairie Oysters were the chosen hangover cure of Concierge since the year dot – or rather since Gomez spotted them in a James Bond movie. Nick preferred the mention of Prairie Oysters in Christopher Isherwood's *Goodbye To Berlin* as a cultural reference, but either way, they seemed to scare off a hangover good and proper. I shuddered at the thought of a gloopy raw egg/brown sauce combo travelling repulsively down my throat.

"Been drinking, Betty?" Pointless question.

"Couldn't sleep after all the excitement so I cracked open the *Twin Peaks* box-set and a bottle of Jägermeister. They don't mix that well, as it happens." She sat down with her mug and viewed me with wide, red eyes. "So? Talked to Nick?" Betty took a sip of her modified Prairie Oyster and tried not to retch. "Still holding out hope for him to give up?"

"Well... "

"Where is he now?"

"Um... "

"Don't tell me he's 'disappeared' again," said Betty.

"Yes and no. I know where he is."

"Somewhere in Swiss Cottage, right?"

I nodded and rubbed my tired face.

"Bill and Amber's. Couple of old rockers. A better class of smack den, to be fair. You take your shoes off as you go in. It's kind of hilarious. It's all gorgeous Heals furniture in there, Celia Birtwell wallpaper... Just as well, they never leave. At least they've got something nice to look at. Anyway, go on."

"We'd agreed to discuss everything properly last night, it was even him who brought it up."

"Oh, you'd better get used to this."

"Plus earlier on he'd walked in on Sam and I... "

"What?" Betty sat up. I twisted with embarrassment. "This is an interesting curveball."

"It was nothing; Sam was in the dressing room, and it might have looked like we were having a bit of a... moment, but... "

Betty cackled. I reluctantly recounted what had happened and more cackling ensued. "This is amazing! I knew about you two. I knew it."

"But Nick... "

"Oh, Sylvie!"

"You don't know what we had."

"I fucking do," said Betty. "I remember it well. It was pretty heavy even when things were good, babe, let's be honest."

"I still love him. I care about what happens to him. I don't exactly feel like celebrating. His face... Seriously, Betty, I could have died."

Before she could speak, my phone vibrated on the kitchen table. I rushed to answer it, praying it was Nick saying he was safe, on his way over. Maybe that was too ambitious. Safe would do. I didn't recognise the number at first and my heart plummeted – only to bungee straight back up when I realised who it was.

"It's Sam," I mouthed, before taking the phone up to the bedroom, leaving Betty to hyperventilate. Once she'd heard the door close she followed me, clutching her necklaces to her chest to minimise jingling and pressed her ear to the bedroom door. She could barely hear anything – Sam was doing most of the talking. As soon as it sounded as if the conversation was wrapping up, Betty crept back into the living room, resuming her position on the sofa and trying to look innocent.

"I thought you said you hadn't given him your number?" enquired Betty as I walked back in.

"It's on the Concierge call-sheet. I could see your feet under the door, by the way."

"I don't know what you mean. Anyway, what did he say?"

I snuggled into my chair and rested my head on the arm. "He just wanted to make sure I was OK. "

"Lovely man."

"And to tell me he's been fired."

"What?" Betty's voice shot up several octaves and she thumped the sofa with her fist.

I pressed my forehead into the comforting plush of the armchair. "Nick called him two hours ago asking him to pick him up, he wasn't capable of driving himself home. Looks like he killed two birds with one stone. Once he'd got him back and practically tucked him in, Nick gave him his marching orders. I feel so responsible, I ... Hang on, where are you going?" Betty was on her feet and slinging her bag over her arm.

"To sort my bloody brother out." She necked the rest of her Prairie Oyster, released a strange yelp of repulsion and slammed the cup on the worktop.

"But... "

"You're coming too." She dragged me to my feet and forced me into a coat. A small scuffle and some shouts of frustration later, victory was Betty's and we were in her car, barrelling over to Richmond. It was a beautiful autumn day, mist hanging low over the Thames. I hardly noticed.

"This is going to look as if I'm on Sam's side," I said as Betty drove. "It's going to make it worse."

"Well, you two need to pull yourselves together anyway, so this is an opportunity."

I hunkered down inside my coat. Betty was right, annoyingly, but all I wanted to do was hide. Nick was hiding, why couldn't I? Why was I the one who had to sort everything out? Nice of him to have called too, I thought petulantly... he'd managed to phone Sam to fire him. I never imagined machismo could be so immune to the effects of smack.

Betty had pulled up outside a juice bar on the high street. "I've never needed a wheatgrass shot more than I do this minute," she muttered. "Want anything?"

I shook my head and attempted a smile. What I wanted couldn't be found in a poncy juice bar. I was so tired I didn't know what I wanted. I didn't know what I could allow myself to feel about anything. If I kept the drawbridge up, I didn't have to commit my feelings either way.

Betty made a great racket of unlocking Nick's door and stormed inside. Nick was easily located by the trail of strewn shoes, coat and bag which led from the hall into the lounge. The TV was blaring and the light was still on, giving the room a depressing hue as the artificial glow did battle with the real deal outside.

Nick was lying on his back on the love-seat, legs hanging over the end, eyes closed, the voices on the TV news surrounding him like a shroud, so loud they were almost tangible. Betty turned down the volume and approached him. I felt a surge of love and hate and despair at the sight of him, the thought of where he'd just come from, the fact I now seemed so low on his list of priorities. He looked horribly still.

"He's not… "

"Dead? No. But he needs water," said Betty, bustling through to the kitchen. I continued to stare at Nick. I had no expectations of him anymore, I'd slowly learnt over the past few spiralling months it was easier not to go down that road. I waved a hand tentatively over his face, pausing slightly under his nose. Just to make sure.

"You're wasting your time with that," I said as Betty came back in with a tumbler of water. "He's out for the count."

"Shouldn't be a problem," breezed Betty, throwing it straight in his face. It took him a few moments before blinking awake. To speed up the process, Betty gave him a hard slap, the empowering effects of righteous anger and Prairie Oyster à la HP sauce really kicking in.

Nick sat up, leaning back on his elbows and squinting at his intruders through dripping hair. It wasn't clear whether he was furious or confused or just completely out of his tree. None of the above were out of the question.

"What the fuck, Betty? This love-seat is an antique." He pulled himself up, surveying the damage and dabbing it ineffectually with his sleeve.

"Never mind that," Betty said. "Explain yourself."

"Sylvie!" he exclaimed, as if only just realising I was there. "Oh God."

"Nice to see you too."

"I mean, you... I... "

"You could have called," I said drily. "I was worried." Understatement of the year.

"I'm sorry," he said weakly, resuming his position on the damp love-seat and closing his eyes again. I waited for more. But that was it. He had no more words to offer me. I wanted to scream but he'd have withdrawn even more. There was nothing I could do, nothing I could control other than my own reactions.

"You'll have to do better than that," said Betty. "And what's all this about Sam?"

Nick opened his eyes slightly, as if he was trying to figure out what she was talking about. "Oh, this morning. Yes, I sacked him," he responded finally. "He wasn't right for the group."

"Because he was nice to your fiancée? Who you're neglecting?" Betty asked, looking into his blood-shot eyes, which now blazed straight back at her.

"It's 'whom'. And anyway, this is none of your business," he said. "Sylvie and I can sort this out between us. Maybe you should leave."

"You might have blocked out everything we went through the first time, but it is etched on my memory and I won't watch you do this to yourself again, you've so much more to lose."

"Will you just go?" Nick repeated, harder this time. Her last sentence pricked something within his conscience but he couldn't listen to her any more. Betty seized her bag and left without another word. The door closed with a slam and she could be seen stomping to her car, pausing only to mouth 'fuck you' at Nick through the window. He closed his eyes again, letting his head sink back. Betty had ultimately done us a favour, but her methods could do with a little fine-tuning.

I knew better than to ask about the debacle with Sam. He'd only be defensive and besides, this was just a symptom of the deeper issue: Nick was increasingly incapable of having a functioning relationship with me, but he didn't want anyone else to have a shot. Not yet. His rational side reminded him constantly that it was a matter of time until something had to change, I'd leave, find someone who could make me happy. Preferably in that order. And there would be nothing selfless about his motives for letting me go – he'd be lonely but not guilty. He wasn't quite numb enough yet to accept this as an option. Getting there though. Definitely getting there.

For me this wasn't only about stability, it was also that no one was exactly having fun here. I wasn't having fun. Nick didn't look like a man having the time of his life. The sycophantic enablers had been encroaching for a while now, in awe of the myth, cool by association in his presence and, evidently, stoking his habit. They all fantasised about being his friends, but they weren't – a friend would have wanted him to get better, protect him from what had nearly ruined his life before. As far as he was concerned, he could barely tell them apart, they were all just unctuous links in the chain that led to a fix. The fact they treated him like royalty just eased the way. When he'd been clean, he'd always been the least approachable member of the group, but drugs were the perfect thing to have in common, the perfect way in to a connection. He was porous, exposed, in constant need, magnetising all the wrong people. Or the right people. It saved him a lot of money. People were happy to exchange drugs for a few hours in the company of a star. Living the dream, baby. He was sleep-walking through the days, carried aloft on a cloud of ego-stroking and hot air and dope. Why should he stop when it was all so easy?

"Do you want a drink?" he said eventually.

"Oh, Nick. I just want you to stop." It was as if someone was speaking through me. But I still couldn't give him an ultimatum. I still couldn't say, "Or I can't marry you." And that was what he needed to hear if anything even stood a chance of changing. He didn't speak or move or look at me. Ire rose through me until it pushed me to my feet. I turned the TV volume up full and left.

*

Half of me needed to get away and think. The other half knew there was nothing to think about. Both halves were united in their need for one thing, however. Raisin toast at the Coffee Cup café, the perfect haven for contemplating life, cheering oneself up, considering the next move. Never was the need for those sweet, buttery little slices so great as it was today. In fact, despite what had just happened, raisin toast was all I could think about.

As I drove north towards Hampstead, I scrolled through the songs on my phone but my staples had been corrupted. Every one of my favourite albums had taken on a new context when Nick and I realised they were *our* favourite albums. We'd marinated ourselves in them and they'd woven us ever more tightly together. Listening to them now was hard. Those songs that had been in my bones before I'd even heard of Nick would never be the same. *Marquee Moon* – my musical rosary, the pure point of light amid the chaos – had to be the exception. It's too powerful to be contaminated. I press play, almost for the sake of experiment, and I can hardly stand to hear the first chords of 'See No Evil'. He's done it. He's ruined it for me. I looked at the album cover on my phone, all cheekbones, unhealthy pallors, amphetamine eyes. Television didn't care, but I just couldn't get over it.

14

"Twelve?" The waiter repeated back to me. "Twelve slices? Like… a whole loaf?"

"That's what I said."

"You're waiting for friends?"

"Nope."

Bloody hell, it was a free country, wasn't it? I should be allowed to enjoy as much toast as I wanted without interrogation. Besides, I hadn't been there in ages; I had some catching up to do. The fact I would be paying nearly thirty quid for a loaf I could basically buy for £1.50, take home and toast for myself didn't put me off. I wedged myself into a wood-panelled corner of the café and took out my phone, fiddling with it intently so that Frosty the Snow-waiter would get the message and rack off.

I clicked on 'recent calls' and was greeted by Sam's number. Almost without thinking, I called it. It was as if forces beyond my control were acting for me. I felt a rush of nerves and considered disconnecting but it was too late, he'd picked up.

"Sam, where are you?"

"At home. Where are you?"

"The Coffee Cup. I don't suppose you… "

"I'll be right over."

When he said he'd be right over he meant it. It felt as if I barely had time to rush to the bathroom to daub on some lip-gloss and brush my hair before Sam came in, looking especially tall within the grotto-like interior of the café. I didn't know whether it was because I'd just seen Nick looking red-eyed and funereal but Sam looked like the healthiest person I'd ever seen, with his white teeth (not too white, not blue white like Gomez's), honey-coloured hair and brown skin that made his blue eyes look even bluer. He looked like a dazzling Viking, too big for his surroundings, infusing everything with sunlight. Everything went a bit slow-mo and hazy, and I realised I was staring. Better say hello at least.

"Hello." Try as I might, I couldn't stop my mouth from wrestling itself into a bit of a beam. I pinched my thigh to snap myself out of it.

"Hello." His eyes flicked up at my face as he pulled up a chair. As he was settling, the waiter came over and presented me with my entire sliced loaf of raisin bread.

"You do have a friend," said the waiter with an accusatory tone. "Will you be wanting raisin toast too? I'm not sure how much bread we have left. "

"We can share," I said, pushing the plate to the middle of the table. Sam looked at it before deciding not to ask. He didn't have to. He wasn't going to complain either – if ever there was a day he felt like hiding out and inhaling a mountain of comfort food…

"May I?"

"Of course, they must have brought all of this by mistake." Sam gave a small smile and took a piece. I took one for myself and tried to nibble it as daintily as I could. I know this wasn't a date, but still, I never really understand why dates often consist of going to restaurants where you have to watch each other eat. It's rarely a good look.

"I'm so sorry about Nick." The words wouldn't stay in any longer. I'd tried to hurriedly plan some small talk but it was too late.

"Don't be," Sam said evenly. "He can't sack me. I spoke to Les and they won't be getting rid of me. This is barely a drama in comparison to the Gomez saga, Les is busy trying to sort all that out as we speak." I was so preoccupied with Nick my brain had just pushed Gomez's kidnapping to one side. It had certainly been quite the weekend.

"Anyway, I haven't done anything wrong," continued Sam. "Not by previous roadies' standards at least. He told me about Dogfish… "

I put a hand up to stop him. "Not while I'm eating."

"And Les said Nick doesn't have the authority to fire anyone while he's in that state. It's like a joke, making someone come and pick you up from a smack den and then firing them. It really is kind of funny."

"Glad you think so," I said. "So… you told Les about that?"

"He'd worked it out anyway. I just have to make sure Nick and I stay out of each other's way, which is fine by me. The man's an idiot."

"Now… "

"OK, he's behaving like an idiot. I'm sorry, but it's true. He doesn't know when he's got it good. Look at what it's doing to you. You're exhausted."

"He's changed so much, Sam. Honestly, it's hard to recognise him sometimes. But I'm kind of all he's got, and he's obviously in pain. Maybe I just need to find another way, try harder."

Sam leant forward and grabbed my hand, making me jump slightly. "You are trying more than most people could or would. If anyone needs to try harder it's Nick, and I'm not sure he's capable."

I fiddled with my napkin, aware Sam was looking straight at me, waiting for my response. And he was right. Betty was right. My own instincts were right – but some flicker of pride just didn't allow me to accept that I'd made the wrong choice. The more people rallied round, the more a small, defiant part of me blindly wanted to prove everyone wrong, to show that I could handle Nick, addict or not, help him if I could. I often wondered whether this drive to rescue Nick had more to do with my pride than my heart. Intertwined with angst and love and even pity were feelings of control-freak doggedness. Leaving him would be tantamount to admitting defeat.

It's funny. You never really know yourself, never know which quality you didn't realise you had will leap to the fore until you're confronted with a situation like this. It was as if life had presented me with a problem I had to conquer, and if that meant staying inside the cell I'd made for myself and watching the walls close in, so be it. No one could say I'd walked away.

"I think I need to go out with him," I said finally. Sam looked at me.

"You already do. That's the problem."

"I mean, I need to go on a date with him. Act as if we're just starting out. That's what people do, isn't it? Sometimes? It might help if we see each other out of context. Then if I walk away, I'll know I tried everything."

"You're wasting your energy. "

"If we're going to be friends I need you to be supportive. Nick and I… "

"Friends?" interrupted Sam. "That goes without saying. I knew I wanted to be your 'friend' the minute we met. Look, whatever you decide to do, I will do my best to respect it. I don't think he deserves you but I'm not going to say anything."

I laughed. "You just did."

"Well, I won't judge, and I'm here if you need me."

I nodded gratefully and gave his hand a squeeze.

"So where are you going to take the Dark Prince on this date then? Not here, please?" he added. "This is our place now, Sylvie, this is where we broke the record for the most amount of raisin toast eaten in one sitting. Does that mean nothing?" And to prove his point Sam took another weary bite out of yet another piece of toast.

"No, not here," I smiled. 'Our place'. He just said it. He'd rushed to my side when I'd called. It was practically like the beginnings of a relationship, which would have been great if I wasn't in one already. Sam was doing everything Nick should have been doing. Nick was kind and loyal and gorgeous and he loved me, but everything was absolutely on his terms. He'd made me feel safe once; he definitely didn't do that any more. And I wasn't sure whether it was wishful thinking but I had the feeling that maybe Sam would always treat me like this if I gave him the chance.

We sat together for hours in the hazy light of the Coffee Cup, barely aware of anyone around us, talking about everything. This was the first time we'd managed to really talk without the conversation being monopolised by the subject of Nick. We talked about our families, our favourite records, places, our heroes (mine: Patti Smith, Molly Parkin, Ian Dury. His: Robert Mitchum, Ronnie Barker, Ian Dury – we agreed to share him), favourite books, teenage crushes… it had turned into an intensive getting-to-know-you session and we were laying all of our shiniest and most interesting cards on the table. It was only when the staff started ostentatiously scraping chairs and crashing about with a Hoover that we realised it was time to go. We'd even finished the toast.

I arrived back home in a sugary dream-state, barely aware of the journey back at all. Switching on lights and turning up heaters, I floated in distractedly. And then I caught sight of the kitchen, which appeared to be a graveyard for Prairie Oyster ingredients.

The reality of my pre-Coffee Cup, pre-Sam day shuttered down in front of me. It was time to call Nick and arrange that 'date'. I might have insisted that this was about reminding him what was at stake, but I also sorely needed reminding why I wanted to make this work. I struggled to remember; sweeter memories having been shunted back by big, dark, new ones. It hadn't taken very long. It was hard to know whether Nick saw this in quite the same way, having slipped willingly into his day-to-day fug, but he'd have to meet me halfway. It felt like I was about to organise our first date, and in a way I was; I was dealing with a different Nick now. Part of me was repelled, part of me still wanted him, and part of me was curious as to who he really was now, and whether we could move forward at all.

Various, more forthright approaches flickered through my mind before I rang him; the kind of approaches Betty would take, or Ange or even Pearl. But heroin had evidently been in his life longer than I had. I'd almost started to feel as if it had more right to him than I did. I was the mistress. If we could get to a place where he wanted to quit by himself, perfect. If not, I'd have to work out whether I liked this new/old Nick enough to stick around at all.

15

"Nick," I said, eyeing myself sternly in the mirror. "I'm calling to see if you want to go on a date."

"I thought you were calling to do the opposite," said the voice on the end of the line.

"No," I replied. Give it time. "But we need to… We need to… you know." It had all started so well. Nick's glum, reedy voice with its Estuary twang just tore me up. Being with Sam had been like turning on a brilliant light that bleached out my feelings for Nick. It made me struggle to see why there was any question as to whether I should leave or not. But as soon as I reconnected with Nick, the feelings of incompleteness without him were back, particularly now part of him seemed so unreachable. It was hard to know how healthy this was, how much of it was just a case of not wanting to be beaten. But I also knew it hadn't been that long since we'd been properly in love, with nothing in the way. Let's face it, I was confused.

"Let's meet at the Swan."

"No." Too easy as always. He didn't mean it but he was used to people working around him. I loved the Swan, but Nick, on the few occasions he did go out, always went there. This was going to be on my terms, and my turf, for once. Let's see if he could manage that.

And so it was arranged. Nick would come to the pub in Strawberry Hill at 7pm the following night. I didn't want to leave it too long in case something changed and he disappeared again. This was not how it was supposed to be; the writers of *The Rules* would have seriously disapproved. But they hadn't written a 'Rules' for the partners of drug addicts, as far as I knew. I could have done with a copy if it had existed. I wasn't exactly being treated like a goddess any more, which magazine columns and self-help books relentlessly tell me is no more than I should expect. But this wasn't a regular situation. I would, however, look like a goddess, and see if that made him realise that he had to treat me better before someone else did.

He was rattled by Sam, so he wasn't made of stone despite outward appearances. A bit of mystery and restraint was surely better than the alternative, I reminded myself (he wasn't hot-tempered like Les, dramatic like Gomez, neurotic like Johnson). But I had to concede that, when in a relationship with a walking Enigma Code Machine, that same emotional opaqueness could also be… well, pretty annoying. In fact, it was mostly annoying. Still, I had to at least try to max out the positive. This was a critical time.

After a night of broken sleep and a day of moisturising, brushing, perfuming and panicking, the time came to slip on my favourite white dress with the bell sleeves and, after a final check in the mirror by the door, I began the walk to the Rose, which seemed to be waiting for me, twinkling expectantly at the foot of the hill. This former old-man pub was now bedecked with fairy lights, 'vintage' lampshades in jewel colours and the sticky, faded carpet had long been discarded in favour of dark, glossy floorboards. Being a Monday night, it was mercifully quiet save for a few regulars getting their pints in before heading to the blues club upstairs. Nick had already arrived, sitting in a booth with a newspaper and two Jack Daniels and Cokes in front of him. He slid one glass across the table as I approached.

"No kiss?"

"Not on a first date," I said, immediately regretting the fact I'd allowed my internal view of tonight seep out. First date with the new, not-so-improved Nick. First date with Nick the addict. He looked at me, lupine, before allowing his face to crack a smile.

"Right… of course. How forward of me." Thank God for that, I thought. He thinks it's a coy little joke. Nick was relieved too. He'd thought this was going to be more of a final date, a 'we need to talk' date. But it was looking as if it might be a 'let's start again' date. Don't get too comfy, sunshine.

"You look good," I managed. I almost said "You look well" but I was glad I didn't, it always sounded forced and loaded, and besides, he didn't. But somehow he had still managed to look good. That heroin chic rubbish in the 1990s had nothing on him. Here was the real deal, for better or worse.

"You look perfect," he replied quietly. "My Sylvie… " Sweet, I thought, trying to ignore the shiver scampering down my back. He was trying to beam out love he could barely express any more; it used to be easier than this, but the message was received. I took a sip and looked at him. His skin was greyer than usual, and his eyes, still a little smudged with eyeliner from the gig two nights ago (he'd never got the hang of cleansing) were a picture of strung-out exhaustion. But he looked handsome, like he'd bothered, and, seeing each other out of context, a rush of renewed attraction fizzed between us.

"So… " His sloe-black eyes glittered at me as I played with my straw. But before he had a chance to say another word, I became aware of a man hovering about in our field of vision, grinning at Nick. He wasn't going away.

"It's you, isn't it? Nick Sinclair!" The man was turning red with excitement. Nick nodded and looked guiltily at me. I smiled with difficulty.

"BARRY!" The red-faced man was shouting over at his friend at the bar, beckoning him over. "BARRY! Look!"

Barry's face lit up. "Fuck me. Duran Duran!"

"No, you cock. It's NICK SINCLAIR! FROM CONCIERGE!" Nick ran a hand through his hair and braced himself. Several chubby men bumbled over one by one, and so it began – the gushing about how they saw Nick in 1988 at the Astoria and it 'changed their life' (I very much doubted it), and does he remember signing Barry's girlfriend's show programme at Reading Festival? And will Gomez and Johnson be joining him? He had to explain that just because they're in a band, doesn't mean they were all 'bezzie pals'. This went on for some time.

I extricated myself to go to the toilet – it was something to do – and by the time I returned yet another Barry was sitting in my seat, staring at Nick. It must have been flattering but basically this is a man having a quiet drink with his partner, is nothing sacred? Nick tried to wrap up the conversation and gestured to Barry Mark Two to get up so I could resume my seat. Finally they started to leave. "You can have him back now," guffawed Fanboy, taking the opportunity to stare at my breasts before moving along. "Look after 'im!" said another. I'm trying to, I thought, baring my teeth at them.

"Is that why you don't take me out on dates then?" I said, once the coast was clear.

Nick grimaced. "Sorry. Let's get another drink."

"I'll go," I said quickly. "Just… hide behind your paper or something."

As I waited for my order, I noticed Nick had managed to conceal himself and was, so far, still alone. But seconds after I'd picked up the drinks and paid, I was approached by two of the men. I knew they were more interested in Nick than they were in chatting me up, but there was a glassy look in their eyes which told me they either expected me to wangle some more time with Nick or…

"How d'you manage that then?"

"Well, I just handed the man some money and in return, he gave me alcohol," I was not in the mood.

"We mean, how did you get together with someone like Nick?" persisted one of the Barrys, failing to get it. "Are you a groupie?"

I took a deep breath. If anyone was behaving like a groupie…

"Well, you bagged Nick at the right time!" said the other Barry. "After the wilderness years, bi-i-i-g old come-back… "

"I know… " I murmured, edging away. Their attempts at familiarity were predictably breeding contempt.

"They'd better not split up again," added Barry the first, spitting accidentally on my top. "Otherwise you'd have to work! Ha!" The entire collective fell about laughing. A woman. With a job. Hilarious notion. Obviously Nick was a meal-ticket, obviously this is the eighteenth century. I shed an internal tear for the Pankhursts.

"Well, this has been fun," I said, witheringly, "but I'd better go, I never normally say anything in public without running it past my fiancé first."

"Cheerio!" said Barry the second. This too was lost on them. I walked back to Nick, picking up bits of low-level Barry conversation, mostly chunnering about Nick or appraising my rear end. As I sat down with the drinks, Nick was saying goodbye to someone called Gram on his phone. Something felt wrong. Already.

"Who was that?" I asked a little too brightly as Nick shoved his mobile into his inside pocket.

"Hm?… Oh, it's someone who needs to drop off some tapes with me. He'll be popping by in a minute. It won't take long." He was tense.

"OK," I said slowly. "When you said tapes, did you in fact mean drugs? You can say yes. Be honest."

"It'll just take a minute." Yes, then. Well, this was all very real. I tried to ignore the twisting in my stomach. Just because he was getting drugs tonight didn't mean he was going to take them tonight. Did it? He wouldn't. Not on our 'date'.

It was difficult for the conversation to take off again after the phone call, as we were now playing a waiting game until this Gram character arrived. I tried to imagine what he looked like, and both of us, for different reasons, glanced edgily towards the door every time someone came through it.

And finally there he was, leering and stomping towards the booth in pink and black brothel-creepers. He was a blur of pin-stripes, mod badges, floppy bleached hair, tattoos. For someone engaged in general dodginess, he sure liked to be conspicuous. I knew it was him the moment he appeared and I loathed him on sight. The oily way he was around Nick, the way he had to be forced to acknowledge me, the cold fish eyes not matching the smiling, flattering gob – it was all abhorrent. He sat next to Nick and stared at me, taking me in. It was hard to tell whether he fancied me or resented me but he gave off a seriously possessive vibe around Nick. And when he headed to the bar to get Gram a drink, his dirty little claws appeared.

"Thing for popstars, then?"

"I have a thing for Nick, which is why we're getting married." No need to let the cracks show to the outside world, especially not to him.

"Nick never mentioned it." I wasn't rising to that. "How did you meet, are you one of those chicks who hangs around at gigs and... "

"Tries to pick up popstars?" I interrupted, seething. "No. You?"

Gram attempted a belittling expression. "I'm not a chick."

So what if I was a 'chick' who went to gigs? What kind of a world did we live in if there was still a stigma around girls who just wanted to go to a gig? "One of those chicks... " The same never applied to men, wheedling their way backstage to slaver over their heroes. One thing was clear here: Gram thought he owned Nick, there was a distinct air of competition and he was threatened by my presence. Maybe he thought I would try to wean him away from heroin – then he'd have one less wealthy client to squeeze dry and boast about.

"So would you say you're a bad girl trying to be good?" he persisted, like a school bully. "Or a good girl trying to be bad? Wait, I think I can guess."

"I work with Concierge. I'm part of the crew."

"The crew?" Gram looked amused. "Making tea, then?"

"Wardrobe," I replied through gritted teeth.

"Really?" Gram looked me up and down and then smirked under his breath. "Bad girl trying to be good."

"Good bad, not evil," I muttered airily. "You, however… "

The tension lifted slightly when Nick returned with a neat Jameson's for Gram, but I wasn't going to let this arsehole off lightly.

"Nick," I began, giving my new nemesis a hard look. "Apparently Gram thought you and I just got together because I was a groupie." Gram shifted.

"Sylvie works with the band, I've told you about her loads of times," sighed Nick, sitting down beside me.

"It was a joke," Gram mumbled. God, he's repulsive, I thought, Nick really must have a problem if he's prepared to hang out with him. But tonight I was going to roll with it. Tonight was the night I would at least get an inkling as to whether I could live with Nick, his problem and everything – everyone – that went with it. It wasn't looking good so far.

"Well, anyway," Gram turned to Nick. "Maybe we should… "

"Yes… Sylvie, give me a couple of minutes." And so they rose and made for the toilet, leaving me, fragrant, sparkly and feeling thoroughly stupid, to my own devices. The pub was filling up and nobody else appeared to be alone except for me. I played with my phone, pretending to read something on the screen. What would I have done in the days before mobile phones? There are only so many times you can read a beer-mat.

Just as a slightly odd young man started sidling up, they returned. Nick's general demeanour didn't appear to have changed in any way. I tried to check out his pupils but it was hard to tell whether there was any difference as his eyes were so dark. Gram looked wired, as if he'd just snorted a fat line of bugle, which he obviously had. Great, I thought. Now he's going to be talking even more shit. And louder too.

"There's this party just up the road. Why don't you come? I can take you there now if you like?" said Gram, all the words merging into one, as Nick sat back down. This was directed at Nick only. Fine. Any party connected to Gram was a party I did not want to be anywhere near, but I also didn't want him dragging Nick away from me, not tonight.

"We've got plans, Gram." Good answer. I wasn't sure what kind of hold, if any, Gram had over Nick and wasn't sure whether he'd go wherever Gram said if there was the promise of heroin at the end of it. I was proud of him. Small mercies. Gram narrowed his eyes, as if this rebuff must be something to do with me. He hugged Nick, ignored me and slouched back into the night.

"He was nice."

Nick squirmed. "I know, he's a creep but… "

"I get it, he has his uses. Nick, it's fine. All I care about is that we're open with each other. I'm not trying to make you change. I take it he's… around a lot at the moment?" I added carefully. Nick nodded. I pushed aside the image of Sam that had popped into my head and pressed on.

Nick, meanwhile, was warily happy that I didn't seem to be going in the direction of ultimatums. I hadn't mentioned the possibility of him giving up, of trying a new rehab clinic. Which was just as well, because he had no intention of doing either.

His fan-radar suddenly twitched and he looked up, noticing two new men at the bar staring at him and talking between themselves, clearly geeing themselves up to go over and speak to him.

"Shall we make a move?" he said, subtly alerting me with an eye movement.

"Oh! Well, only if you feel you've had enough adoration for one night."

"Not quite enough from you."

"Let's go," I said, chugging back my drink and taking Nick by the hand, keen to avoid a repeat of the earlier super-fan experience. I understood why Nick was so gracious; they bought the albums, saved up for the tickets, supported the group when they were well past their peak. But did they have to be such train-spotters about it? So many fans were in love with the 'rock 'n' roll-ness' of these guys, so why did they have to be so un-rock 'n' roll, prizing bits of paper with scribbled names on, filing away dates of gigs from years ago inside their heads like they were collecting stamps? If they really wanted to hang out with a star, holding a conversation about something other than painstaking details about album covers that even the band themselves either couldn't remember or didn't give two shits about would give them a head start. Still, I'd sooner sit with the biggest Concierge anoraks in town than spend another minute with…

"Gram?" There he was, hopping about in front of Nick's car like a ten-year-old that needed the toilet. "Have you been out here this whole time?" asked Nick. I hung back, my aversion to this man creating a forcefield that was almost visible.

"Um… " He was hinting for something.

"Do you want a lift?" I could have kicked Nick. KICKED him.

"Well, I was going to go to this party, wasn't I? It's only in Twickenham… if you wouldn't mind?" He just had to hijack our night. If he doesn't manage to persuade Nick to 'come in for a bit' it'll be a miracle.

After a journey that consisted of Gram talking non-stop at Nick, who drove with a stare that could break the windscreen, I interrupted the barrage. This area looked familiar, and it didn't have the best associations.

"Isn't this where Dogfish used to live?" I asked carefully. Dogfish was, as you may now have deduced, the notorious former Concierge roadie who racked up an impressive list of indiscretions, all under the influence of mind-bending drugs, before eventually getting sacked. My first day working with Concierge was etched on my mind as the day Dogfish lurched after me into the ladies' toilets begging me to supply him with either heroin or "a snog". He received neither but persisted long into the evening, to the point that Nick had to set up his own gear because Dogfish was busy trying to wear me down. In the opinion of most of Concierge, trying to tell Dogfish to do his job was more trouble than it was worth. It was easier to do it yourself.

"Just here on the right," said Gram.

"I remember," shuddered Nick.

"No, I mean, can you stop here on the right?"

"Oh… " Nick and I were thinking the same thing. The party wasn't at Dogfish's place, surely? Thank God we're just dropping this prick off.

"Why don't you come in for a bit?"

There it is. Nick hesitated. "As I say, we've got plans."

"Just a few minutes?" It was never just going to be a few minutes. I waited. I wasn't going to stop Nick or guilt-trip him, I was just going to see how this unfolded, either way. This had, at least partly, become an experiment; I couldn't let my feelings get in the way yet.

Nick looked at me with an unreadable expression. I shrugged back at him. He knew what the right answer was.

"Maybe just for a few minutes," he said finally. That would be the wrong answer.

I felt some relief as Gram pressed a doorbell other than the one grimily marked 'DOGFISH', but as we mounted the rubbish-strewn stairs to the top floor it became clear from the sound of guttural roaring, swearing and crashing from behind the door that the man himself was very much in attendance.

As Gram pushed the door open, it transpired that Dogfish was the only one 'partying' in the traditional sense (ie. roaring, swearing, crashing). The other guests – of which there were four – were arranged on rotten-looking sofas amid a sea of detritus and were respectively rocking, staring, talking incessantly to no one and, purportedly, sleeping. It was like one of Hogarth's renderings of a desolate London flop-house. Everything looked dark, and there I was in the middle of it like a beacon, excruciatingly shiny and clean.

There were so many things I wanted to say to Nick. I chose to say nothing. It wouldn't have made any difference. I froze as Dogfish spotted me, lumbering over with open arms, growling something obscene under his toxic breath. Nick quickly moved between us and administered a skilful hug-come-push, redirecting him towards the bomb-site of a kitchen. He then closed the door behind Dogfish, who was apparently quite happy; he didn't bother coming out again. As soon as he'd been shoved out of the way, the sound of the room presented itself: a blend of yammering, creaking voices and *Dusty in Memphis* crackling from the record-player, an incongruous soundtrack of nostalgic sweetness and shimmer, a distant light at the end of a very dark tunnel.

"Who's hosting this knees-up, then?" I asked, looking around me. 'Knees-up'. The mental picture did not correlate with what was actually happening here. There was no likelihood of anyone breaking into a jubilant Cockney song and dance routine. I wasn't sure whether my fellow guests even had the chutzpah to make it to the bathroom.

"Carmel's," responded Gram, sitting down next to a cadaverous character so grey he practically blended in with the colourless furniture. As if on cue, a pale woman, around fifty, staggered in from the bedroom. Carmel herself, bedecked in full Mod regalia. Considering the obsessive care Mods generally take over their appearance… well, I guessed this was what happened when you swapped amphetamines for opiates. Her black Mary Quant shift was creased and her white tights stained and laddered. The look was topped off by smudgy black rings of eye make-up and a woolly black bob which rose at the back, either through back-combing or just through never being brushed. But she was benevolent and I was glad to be in the presence of another woman.

"Good to meet you. Sylvie," I said, extending a hand.

"No, Carmel." She was confused but took my hand limply.

"No, sorry… I meant, I'm Sylvie," I murmured, losing the will. But the ghostly woman seemed happy with the arrival of someone from the outside world, as if I'd brought a bit of it in with me. She didn't look like she left the flat very often.

"Take a seat," she said, gesturing listlessly. Nick and I attempted to squash ourselves into the same mouldy armchair. There was nowhere else free. Our gracious hostess then offered cocaine as if it were an aperitif.

Nick silently fumbled in his wallet for a note. "I'm all right, ta," I replied. "Wouldn't mind a cup of tea."

"Really?" This was an event. And, let's be real here, I was being bloody-minded. Apart from anything else, this was exactly the kind of situation that would have been infinitely more fun with the assistance of a few toots. I could see how this kind of thing could go; it was an interesting catch-22. But tonight I would not step through that portal. Tonight I was making a point to Nick. Tonight I would tolerate but not participate. That was the idea. Would he notice? Would he fuck.

"You don't want uppers? Downers?"

Uppers sounded good… "Just tea."

"Right. Tea… " Carmel disappeared into the kitchen. I knew I wasn't ever going to see that tea.

Gram suddenly got up. "Can I talk to you for a minute, Nick?"

Nick looked up from the jewel case in his hand. As I watched him mutely get up and leave me in the living room of the damned, watched him walk like an automaton into the bedroom and shut the door, I wondered at what point it could have possibly felt like a good idea to 'see how this plays out'. To know I was standing by as my fiancé was almost definitely about to shoot up in the next room with a man who didn't exactly have his best interests at heart felt bizarre and wrong. Couldn't I stop him? Should I just leave? He was a grown man. Urgent thoughts swirled but I was rooted to the spot.

The cadaver on the sofa came to life, weakly offering a home-made crack pipe. I appreciated the gesture. It was fashioned badly from an old brandy miniature, still jagged. I'd be inhaling more glass dust than anything else. I demurred. By the time Gram opened the bedroom door again over half an hour later, I'd been adopted by one of the only other guests who was not asleep, and was listening to an exhausting rant about his relationship with a temperamental pet rat. I was starting to reconsider that pipe. Someone flipped the record and dropped the needle onto 'The Windmills Of Your Mind'.

"Sylvie, can you come here?"

"Why?"

"Nick wants you."

"I'm here," I stonewalled. Nick didn't need an envoy to summon me. "Anyway, I'm in the middle of a conversation with... sorry, what was your name?"

"Spooky Dave," said my companion.

"With, um... Spooky Dave. So... "

"Just come here." I rose, heading reluctantly for the dim, plum-hued bedroom. I could smell that same burnt sweetness that I smelt under the door in Nick's house that afternoon with Sam. When my eyes adjusted to the semi-darkness, I saw that Nick had already nodded out on the bed. I could hear Dusty's silvery voice calling me back from the other side of the door.

"You said he wanted to talk to me. He's out fucking cold." I prodded the prone body on the bed.

"Don't worry, I interrupted your fascinating conversation with good reason."

"Don't," I said. "That man sounded like he hadn't had a conversation with someone for a long time. He was talking as if his life depended on it."

"He's on crack, goes with the territory," said Gram, moving in front of the closed bedroom door. I could still hear Spooky Dave prattling in the other room. "OK, *I* want to talk to you."

I looked at his silhouette in the darkness; it was like looking at a shadow. I could hear Nick breathing behind me. I may as well have been alone. "Does this always happen?"

"What?"

"The comatose thing. I don't have much experience... "

"Everyone's different, but yeah, it's got soporific qualities, that's kind of the point. Why? Curious?" He took a step closer. I couldn't tell whether he was joking.

"Not really." Little too close now. Maybe if I didn't look into his fishy eyes then everything would be OK. Then I became annoyed at myself for even thinking that, for giving him so much power. He wasn't Satan. He was just a slimy hanger-on. A hanger-on with Nick in the palm of his hand.

"He's been really concerned about you… " And a hanger-on who apparently was a closer confidante to Nick than I was. Concerned about me? This I had to hear.

Gram continued calmly, like a doctor. He moved to sit by the bed, his acidic breath greeting my nostrils. "Since he started using again there's been an understandable separation between the two of you."

"It had not escaped my notice," I replied, echoing his formal tone. This was such a joke on so many levels.

"I can help you bond."

"Oh, piss off, Gram. This is none of your business."

"On the contrary," he continued, surreally business-like. "As his supplier, I do take some responsibility."

"So?"

"Well, he's not going to give up." He started chopping out a line of powder on a CD case on the bedside table. "But there is an alternative." He stood up and held the case towards me. "Come on, bad-girl-trying-to-be-good, give up the act."

I squinted at it in the dark. A line of coke was one thing.

"Her-o-in… " crooned Gram, attempting to approximate the tune of the Velvet Underground song of the same name. He was no Lou Reed, that was for sure. On he sang, wavering off key as he moved the jewel case closer.

"After you."

"Doesn't agree with me."

"Funny, that."

He held it even nearer. "China-white," he confirmed, as if it made any difference to me. "Very pure. Just inhale a bit. It's better than sex, better than an orgasm. You'll never look back."

"That's what I'm worried about."

"Don't be a prude," he urged, trying to find another button to press. "Nick does it."

"Yes, he's a great advert for it."

"But it would change everything if you were both using. You'd see everything with a new perspective. You could be together all the time," he continued, a proper snake in my Garden of Eden. "No more lying or disappearing. Just try it." He was lifting the case closer with one hand and lightly taking hold of my wrist with the other, pulling me in a little. I clenched my fist against his creeping gentleness. He'd reckoned on the wrong woman if he thought he could pull his smack-svengali routine on me, but he persisted. "It's perfect. Why would James Brown have written a song called 'King Heroin' if it wasn't?"

"You need to listen to the words, mate." I knew that song better than him, evidently. But here it was, the subject of it, literally under my nose. I was momentarily transfixed by the powder that had so much to answer for, gazing at its enticing, snowy faux innocence, bright with promise, a tiny streak of clean, white light against the dinginess of the room.

"You have it if it's so fucking amazing. Don't waste it on me. Knock yourself out." No really, I wanted to say. Knock yourself out. For everyone's sake. Before someone does it for you.

He laughed. "I told you, it doesn't like me." *That makes two of us,* I thought. "Anyway, this isn't about me. I'm thinking of you. It'll fix everything. You'll be on the same wavelength again. Isn't that what you both need?"

I'd once heard of a film director who'd died at his own party from snorting China-white once. Just once. He'd thought it was cocaine. I always remembered that. I wished Nick would wake up. But what if he did nothing? Then a dreadful thought gripped me. What if it was his idea? It couldn't be.

"Nick…" I pushed him in the side in a bid to rouse him. He was unresponsive. He hadn't let me down tonight; he'd pretty much come up with the goods. I'd wanted honesty, no rose-tint, no expectations, no pressures to change, just a preview of the reality and my possible future. The trailer. He'd shown me exactly what I'd needed to see, with none of the edges knocked off. I just hadn't expected to see it so soon.

I turned back to Gram, still staring at me, willing me to 'just inhale', lifting it a centimetre closer. I felt anger surge.

"Fuck you," I spat, snatching my bag and making a move towards the door. I felt a hand grab me by the back of the neck, pulling my head back and towards the powder. A cocktail of adrenaline, panic and wrath flooded through me. I blew hard on the jewel case, leaving Gram swearing and coughing in a blinding cloud of expensive star-dust. "Just inhale," I yelled as I ran through the nightmarish obstacle course of the flat. "It's better than sex."

17

"Christ ALMIGHTY."

Two shrieked words, followed by the sound of something smashing, rang through an open office window in Soho. It was Les, narrowly avoiding an aneurysm, destroying whatever breakables were left in Concierge's London office with a bo staff. Actually they only had a London office, but to sound more like an international concern, it was always referred to as 'the London office', as opposed to the LA office, the New York office, the Tokyo office. This was show business, remember? The business of show.

Ordinarily, a scene such as this would prompt a visit from the local constabulary, but being Soho, things were smashed and profanities bellowed as a matter of course. Between the crashes came the well-meaning strains of *The Best of Neil Diamond*, an album Les always turned to when he needed to calm down. It never worked.

"Everything all right?" A wizened face appeared at the door. It was Louis, the elderly, Paco Rabanne-scented tailor who rented the rooms upstairs. Les grimaced. He hated Paco Rabanne. Not as a person, you understand, just the aftershave.

"It's just... I just... " His voice faltered at the sight of Les's livid features. "I left my lucky mug in here and I just wanted to take it back before you... "

SMASH!

"Ah." His pointy face fell.

"It's bad luck to believe in luck," growled Les. "Don't trap yourself with superstitious bilge. I did you a favour there."

Louis gripped the ends of the tape measure that hung around his neck and tried again. "Um… so is everything all right?"

"Oh yes!" shouted Les, scanning the room wildly. Louis smiled anxiously and his face disappeared from the crack in the door, his footsteps on the wooden stairs diminishing in volume as he returned to the safety of his office.

Everything was not all right. After barely recovering from the weekend, the kidnapping, the police questioning, discovering one of his charges is shooting up like it's going out of fashion and, of course, the humiliation of appearing on stage in a Viking helmet and being attacked by Concierge fans, it was now Wednesday, and after three and a half days of trying to track down Gomez and Carly and liaising with the police, Les had had a breakthrough. Gomez had contacted him. Good news, you might think.

'EMERGENCY BAND MEETING TODAY, 4pm. BE AT THE LONDON OFFICE WITHOUT FAIL, OR I WILL ACTUALLY KILL YOU. ALL THE BEST, LES.' *That should do it,* he thought, sending texts in shouty capitals to every member of the group and key members of the crew. He then fell into his office chair, wheeled it to the stereo and cranked up 'Sweet Caroline'. Then he glided to the drinks tray – the only thing other than the stereo and Neil Diamond that was always safe from the bo staff – and poured a measure of Laphroaig as he waited for the phone to beep with responding texts. He'd already called Pearl and relayed the news but had furiously hung up when he discovered Gomez had already contacted her that morning.

After having his suspicions about Nick's current condition confirmed by Sam, Les prudently texted Betty in case he failed to show. (Incredible as it may seem, he was sensitive enough not to bother me after Sam had filled him in. There was a heart underneath that psychotic exterior.)

Four o'clock came and went. Everyone, with one notable exception, rolled in at around 5.30pm, as expected. Les had calmed down by this point; now he just felt cynical rather than homicidal. Maybe a little drunk. Neil Diamond had been on repeat for some hours now. Johnson wrinkled his nose when he heard 'You Don't Bring Me Flowers' kick in and walked over instinctively to turn it off.

"STAY AWAY FROM NEIL," shouted Les, quivering a cautionary fist. Johnson made a 'W' sign with his hands to signify 'Whatever'. (He'd picked it up from watching *Skins* in a bid to stay in touch with the 'yoof', and preferably improve his chances with the 'yoof' too. Female yoof, to be specific, although rumour had it that he adopted a 'beggars can't be choosers' take on the situation and shared himself with whoever would have him. He preemptively combatted any questions over his sexuality by being volubly homophobic. Even so, his constant over-compensation meant that at least some of the sharper members of the Concierge family were just waiting for him to come out.)

"Where's Nick?" asked Abra. Sam and Betty exchanged a glance.

"Indisposed," said Les immediately, opening up his laptop in front of him, his brow furrowed. He'd deal with Nick later.

"So what's the emergency?" said Johnson. Les turned his laptop around to face the assembled crowd.

"New screen-saver?" said Betty, squinting at the computer. "I can't make it out. Oh! Oh, I say! And why, pray, would you want to show us a picture of…"

"Eh? Oh, shit. Not that." Les tapped a few things into the keyboard as he logged into Skype. After a few more seconds of fiddling, beeping and ringing, he turned the screen back around to face its audience, prompting a collective gasp. He had another quick glance just to make sure it wasn't his screensaver again.

"Gomez!" yelled Johnson. "Oh man, are you OK? What's going on? Has she... hurt you?" He sounded slightly hopeful. Les gave an ironic smile and shook his head. He knew what was coming, and he knew the rest of Concierge would hate it as much as he did.

"No. I'm quite happy thanks." Gomez smiled beatifically.

"Your hair looks different," said Abra.

Gomez patted his locks. "Carly doesn't have quite the same range of conditioners as I do. But it's fine."

"Stockholm syndrome," murmured Sam.

"I heard that," said Gomez, hardening. "I can assure you it's nothing of the sort."

"She's making him say this stuff!" shouted Johnson.

"I do have a mind of my own." Someone sniggered. "And I have wonderful news."

"He's pregnant!" whispered Betty under her hand, aware Gomez could see as well as hear them.

"Maybe with a beer baby," snorted Les.

"Carly and I have reawakened our relationship," Gomez continued serenely. "And we're starting our own musical project. It's called Aviary – inspired by Wings... you know, when Paul McCartney got his wife to sing and play keyboards... "

"We know about Wings," snapped Abra.

"And it's also inspired by the fact that Carly basically... erm... well, took me hostage. So you know, Aviary, birds in captivity... Anyway, she plays banjo and I play maracas. I mean, she can't actually play, but it's not about being 'perfect'. We're above that, that's the point." He left a pause for reaction but nobody spoke. He continued.

"The music's a new take on the madrigal, crossed with Meatloaf and a sprinkling of Steeleye Span. And we'll both sing; in fact one of the many things I've learned during the past few days is that Carly is a fine Mongolian throat singer."

"Throat-singing?" said Abra. "I've heard that before. It just sounds like someone doing a massive burp down a didgeridoo."

Johnson folded his arms. "Three and a half days and you've already forgiven her?"

"It was all for art," said Gomez. "Which I totally respect. Now, I know this might come as a shock but this has the potential to turn into something special. What I'm trying to say is… the thing is… "

"Just say it," urged Les.

"I'm leaving Concierge to concentrate on Aviary."

Les regarded the rest of the room with a sadistic leer. He'd heard all this before. Now it was their turn to react. And they couldn't. Everyone looked at Johnson, the only original member of the band present in the absence of Nick. Finally he spoke. "I think you've made the right decision," he said, his arms tightening across his chest.

"What?" said Les in a vicious whisper. This was unexpected. "What about the fucking European fucking tour next fucking month?"

"Really, Johnson? I'm so glad you understand," said Gomez, slightly put out that his old band-mate wasn't going to fight for him. He decided to launch into his rehearsed speech. "Well, I'm going to miss you all, but when the time comes to— "

"Gomez? Shut up. If you think whatever tripe you're going to peddle with Carly is worth more than three decades with Concierge, then our respective directions going forward are very different. In other words, BUGGER OFF. JUDAS!" And with that, Johnson burst into tears and crashed out of the room.

"So… what about the tour?" said Abra.

Gomez shrugged. "Sorry."

"Fucking hell," said Les. "Do I even get my £1000 back? It'll be all the more necessary now you're doing us out of a load of work."

"Sorry?"

"The £1000 taken by Carly when she was pretending to be Henson Bedges and putting the wind up us all. Or have you forgotten all of that? I suppose you must have done, it's been three whole fucking days after all."

"Oh… I'll have to speak to her. She wanted to use it to set up Aviary… Maybe you could use it as a tax write-off?"

"I could use it for plenty of other things too. I want my cash, you cowardly prick."

"She can be very forceful… " whispered Gomez.

"So can I. I know where you are," warned Les. And with that, he brought his fist down on the keyboard and disconnected the call. Everyone stared at the blank screen.

"Do you really know where they are?" asked Sam.

Les wheeled over to the whisky bottle again. "Nope."

"What are we going to do?" said Abra. "We're all out of a job!"

"Far from it," said Les after another empowering sip of Laphroaig. "We are going to find ourselves a shit-hot replacement."

Abra looked up. "You're joking. Then Nick and Johnson will be the only two original members of the group left. The fans won't like it."

"Don't underestimate me. As soon as Gomez gets an inkling he's not irreplaceable, he'll be back in the fold. Plus it wouldn't hurt to leak the odd rumour to the press. The whole palaver will generate a truck-load of publicity."

"And what about Nick?" asked Sam.

"What about him? Doubt he'll have much of an opinion on Gomez's new musical venture, if that's what you mean."

"I mean, will he be, erm… fit for the tour?"

"I appreciate your concern," said Les, veins twitching in his forehead, "but Nick always seems to manage to be… well enough to work. Dr Theatre. He's a professional."

He'd make damn sure Nick would be 'well enough'. It was only during downtime that Nick seemed susceptible to old temptations, and while Les wasn't yet sure just how bad Nick was, he was certain he'd pull himself together in time for the tour the following month. He'd make him if he had to. Sometimes

Les felt as if he was the only one who remembered they were all getting older, and that this pop lark wasn't going to last forever. There they all were, acting as if they had all the time in the world, like teenagers who thought they were invincible. Who had to pick up the slack when things went wrong? He did. It made him sick.

After being shooed back into the street, Abra linked arms with Betty and, accompanied by Sam, they headed to the Coach and Horses, a favourite Concierge hang-out. It was early enough to have beaten the office workers to the bar and for a while at least, the pub was all theirs, with just the pen and ink caricatures of Jeffrey Bernard for company.

"What is up with Nick?" asked Abra, pensively sipping a Black Velvet.

"Well... " Sam looked at Betty to gauge how economical with the truth he should be. "It's hard to say. Incidentally, what is that?"

"Guinness and champagne. I'm trying to acquire a taste for it," said Abra. "Don't change the subject. What's going on?"

"He's back on H," said Betty. Sam stared at her in shock. He hadn't discussed this with her but he'd been fairly sure they were going to try to be discreet. "Oh come on, he's my brother. And Abra's one of us."

The straw fell out of Abra's mouth. "God, Betty. That's bad. How's Sylvie?"

"Pretty messed up, as you'd expect," said Betty. "I haven't been able to get hold of her for the past few days, which worries me."

"Maybe we should go and see her," suggested Abra, stirring her drink with her straw.

"Bit much turning up en masse," said Betty, before turning her gaze back to Sam. "But you should."

I wasn't sure how long I'd been lying in bed with the curtains drawn, surrounded by scrunched-up tissues, empty brandy miniatures and torn bits of paper. Between dozes, I'd been flimsily attempting to construct a letter to Nick. My attempt to drink all of the miniatures I'd collected from the various flights we'd been on over the past eighteen months had been more successful, and I drifted off into frequent unsatisfying slumbers before coming back round, remembering the reality and feeling everything ache even more. Then I'd try to write, give up, start drinking, nod off again and so the cycle continued until the tears ran out and I just stared, not quite asleep or awake.

Nick had been calling repeatedly – all or nothing as usual – and again, I was ignoring him. I had no idea what to say. I had to say something, and when that happened it was going to be momentous, but I couldn't dilute the power of that by speaking before I was ready. Fortunately the temptation to talk to Nick wasn't great thanks to the psychic wounds left over from the other night. Pen and paper was the best I could do in the meantime.

It was only when the call of nature became impossible to ignore that I hauled myself out of bed, scattering tissues and bottles as I went. I approached the bathroom mirror gingerly. It was then that I saw not only the inevitably terrifying apparition that was my head – smudgy and teary and crowned with wild bed-hair – but I also caught sight of my new Wonder Woman calendar clock (a recent gift from Betty) for the first time in two whole days and three nights. This nonsense had to stop, instructed my inner school-ma'am. Right now.

I brought my iPod into the bathroom and scrolled through the albums to find something sufficiently eighties. Eighties music cheered me up and made me feel kind of Christmassy (festive and happy, rather than argumentative and bloated). At a time like this, I had to bring out the big guns. I clicked on *Let's Dance* and bravely returned to the mirror of truth.

"Bloody hell," I murmured, tugging a brush through defiant knots of hair and preparing to embark on a face and body overhaul of industrial proportions. On paper, spending forty-eight decadent hours under the duvet sounded luxurious and tempting. Whenever I'd imagined such things, usually when I was at my most busy and sleep-deprived, I definitely dreamed of something a little more Rita Hayworth. Perfumed candles, a constant supply of champagne and peach juice and stacks of old movies to while away the hours as I nibbled chocolates from a heart-shaped box in a pair of pink silk pyjamas. Maybe there'd be some big, blowsy red roses in a vase from a secret admirer, complete with a cryptic note that I would peruse from time to time. I, naturally, would look fabulous. Perfect chestnut hair tumbling down my shoulders in glossy waves, skin velvety and flushed with romance, airbrush-perfect... Or at the very least I wouldn't be rocking the kind of look that would frighten a police horse.

But this... this was worse than being stuck in bed with flu. In fact I'd have preferred it. With a bit of patience and a lot of hot drinks and vitamin C, flu does tend to go away. You know where you are with flu. I didn't know where I was with this situation. In fact there were moments over the past meandering hours that I didn't know where I was full stop.

There was no champagne for a start – not that I felt like

celebrating – and no roses. But there was an admirer, and he wasn't being particularly cryptic, which was just as well. I was tired of trying to work things out. Trying to maintain a relationship with Nick had recently resulted in the development of such honed skills of deduction regarding whereabouts, reasons for silences and indecipherable text messages that I'd have given Poirot a run for his money. I reckoned Poirot probably had a better time too, implausibly frequent murders notwithstanding.

As I sat in the bath, letting my fingers get wrinkly to the sound of 'China Girl', the clouds parted just slightly, and I thought of Sam, something I had barely dared to do up until now. Embracing even the idea of him seemed tantamount to pushing Nick further away, breaking the fragile fibres that still held us together. However, although I barely noticed it, the hard little crystals of guilt that had been building inside me were starting to dissolve and I allowed myself to think of him, and think, and think…

The conclusion of *Let's Dance* meant the conclusion of my bath, I'd told myself, and I dutifully stepped out of the cooling water and swathed myself in towels. A quick return to the mirror and I was already looking better. I slicked on some Gucci body lotion (normally saved for when I was going somewhere special, but I was being forcefully nice to myself), and just at a crucial moment of slathering, I heard a gentle knock at the front door. *Maybe it's Sam*, I thought. *It's probably Betty. But maybe it's Sam…*

After a moment of turmoil – I pulled on my robe, satin clinging to my lotion-wet skin, and made my way barefoot to the door. "Be Sam," I whispered to myself, barely able to look at the glass panel in the door in case I saw Betty's red bouffant instead of Sam's thick, blond hair. "Be Sam, be Sam, be Sam… "

It was Nick. Fuck. The nausea was back. As soon as I saw his dark shape through the frosted glass I almost considered turning away and hiding out, but I couldn't. I'd always believed everything happened for a reason and at the right time, even if it didn't feel like it. And it didn't feel like it, not even slightly. But the fact Nick had come round to my place at all was significant. I always went to him.

"An apology is in order," said Nick, drifting into the living room like a phantom. His face was impassive but he looked as if he was searching for someone, checking if we were alone. His voice was strained, but I'd become used to his inexplicable waxings and wanings.

"Forget it. I'm not looking for one." My voice sounded odd. I hadn't used it for a while.

Nick let his powerful eyes burn into me for a few seconds. "I meant from you."

"From… me?" Life certainly had a fondness for throwing curveballs my way, but this one was a doozy.

"Gram told me what happened." He paced like a caged wolf, glancing about distractedly. I looked at him, waiting. "He said you went off with some guy… "

"This is a joke, right?"

"He'd better not be here now. I mean, you've obviously just got out of bed. You smell all… nice."

I struggled to speak, the colour in my cheeks draining. I knew Gram was a waste of organs the minute I'd laid eyes on him but this was really something. "Nick, he is lying to you. How could you even think he'd be telling the truth?"

Nick shook his head and sat on the sofa, staring at his own fist as it clenched and unclenched. "I know that all of this has been hard on you, but… "

"It didn't happen!" My voice was cracking in disbelief. "Gram grabbed me, he tried to force me to take heroin, did he tell you that? And believe me, out of all of the things I might have dared to hope for that night, running out of a crack den – on my own – was not one of them."

Nick looked up at me, his brows knitted in tension. "Why would Gram lie?"

"Seriously? Come on, Nick, he wants you to himself. It'd be

perfect if it wasn't for me. I've run this through so many times in my head it's driving me mad. This is the first time I've left my bed for two days— "

"I know the feeling… "

"Different reasons. Don't even try to compare it." I started preparing tea angrily. I had to do something constructive with my hands. He didn't deserve a cup of tea, but he was damn well getting one. In the face, if he wasn't careful.

"I wondered why you hadn't answered your phone. I'd assumed you'd cracked and gone off with someone else," said Nick dully. "Wouldn't have blamed you, I suppose."

I looked at him. "I guess that would have made it easier for you, splitting up? You were quick to believe Gram, weren't you? Believe Gram and there's no more guilt, no more worrying about what this whole mess is doing to me."

"I just thought it made sense. I knew it was a matter of time before you gave up on me."

"I might change my mind but that's not giving up, it's called having some self-respect."

Nick warmed his hands on his tea and said nothing.

"What worries me is your lack of reaction over that snake trying to force drugs on me. And the way he was talking, anyone would think you'd discussed it: 'Nick is very concerned… you can bond if you're both using.'" I was fuming at the memory, at having to go back to that place. He just leant forward and sighed.

"Nick?"

"No, it's terrible, he shouldn't have done that." He sounded like he was reading from an autocue.

"Nick? You didn't… this wasn't something you were aware of?"

"Well… it had come up."

"What?" My temperature dropped.

"I didn't know what to do! But what he did was wrong," he

said quickly. "I never said it was something I definitely wanted." Something died, and even though there was so much to say I just had no words left. My body reacted for me, shuddering, a retch rising in my arid throat. Silently I walked to the front door and opened it, pulling my robe tighter around me with my spare hand.

"Get out," I said, swallowing hard. I was granting Gram's wish, which was the last thing I wanted to do. I was removing the ultimate obstacle, but I had to look after myself. This wasn't about pride or defeat any more; this was self-preservation.

Nick remained seated, gazing at me, his head falling softly to one side. "Come on, Sylvie, don't."

"I mean it."

"I was just trying to find ways to make us closer," he persisted, getting up and walking towards me. "It was completely the last resort… "

"The last resort?"

"I wanted you to understand me." This was like a bad dream. What had happened to the man I'd loved? And whose idea was it to replace him with this moron? He had less of a grip on reality than I ever thought possible. And as someone who works with musicians, I was lenient on that scale already. "Go, please. Don't you dare come any closer."

"I have to if I'm to get to the door."

"Well, don't come any closer than you have to." Finally he left, without protestation, just another meaningless apology as he sloped away like a melancholy ghost that had frightened his chosen hauntee too many times. I closed the door before I could see him look back.

It was amazing how much carnage could be created without doing or even moving very much, I thought, surveying the state of the bedroom. My mind, determined to push through what had just happened, did battle with my body, unsure whether I could tackle it. But after cramming an energy bar into my mouth, swiping on the lipstick that made me look slightly less like a dead person and prudently selecting the right CD – an aspirational Janet Jackson one that was rarely played except in genuine emergencies – I was soon gathering up tissues and bottles and plunging them into plastic bags, humming absent-mindedly to the music. I'd turned it up loud enough to drown out my inner monologue. It seemed to be working.

Subliminally, I was also drowning out the fact that there might not have been an inner monologue. I felt absolutely numb, exhausted. My brain had been working overtime and could have been forgiven for taking the opportunity for a bit of respite now Nick was technically gone. I didn't have to analyse what this meant and that meant; this was my decision. His turn to wrangle.

It all felt like it had happened so quickly, putting what was once 'Sylvie and Nick' out of its misery, like resorting to Dignitas, only cheaper, and without the biscuits and Alpine scenery. It wasn't that sudden a split; more of a slow fade than a power-chord finale, even though an unexpected sting in the tail had hastened the end. But while I was the one who chose to cut loose, the psychological cords between us were more resilient than I'd imagined. It would take some serious hacking at those, and probably some sessions with Betty and her Native American smudge sticks. Maybe even some shamanistic shrieking and drumming. But right now I felt as if a dark cloud had already dissipated (or at least skulked back to Richmond) without any drum-whacking at all, and only minimal shrieking. Every cell in my body had sprung into vigorous life again, and my head felt lighter. This could have been down to a period of intensive brandy consumption on an empty stomach, of course.

I smoothed the bed covers and gave the white lacy eiderdown a final tweak. My phone, groaning with messages and missed calls, popped out of one of the folds, in sore need of attention after being ignored for too long. I ignored it again. A few more hours wouldn't kill it. And anyway, my first priority was making some toast and Marmite. Liz Hurley flashed through my mind, as she always did when that little jar beckoned. I was haunted by an interview quote of La Hurley's, putting her cellulite-free limbs down to shunning such luxuries as toast and the black stuff. (She also swore by cold showers – but I'd tried that and had long since decided that cold showers could do one).

Today I would push thoughts of undimpled Sloanes firmly out of my mind. Had Liz ever felt like this? Then I remembered Hugh Grant and Divine Brown and assumed she probably had. Maybe that would have been an extenuating toast and Marmite situation. I just kept on spreading – lightly, mind (Marmite-haters, in my opinion, were people who merely over-spread) – giving an occasional glance towards my phone as it charged. The pre-split messages from Nick, like a sad whisper from the past, would need deleting. Messages from Les and from Betty would need to be faced. Just not yet.

I barely allowed myself to hope there might be a message from

Sam, although a small voice inside insisted I was allowed to hope freely for such things now, even if it did still feel a little wrong so soon after the unholy cremation of my relationship with Nick. There was another tap at the front door – and I paused, toast-crumbs still clinging to my lips.

An Interflora card was on the mat, indicating that a delivery was in the porch – and so there was: a wild arrangement of pink and orange tiger-lilies nestling in a cobwebby corner, dotting the carpet with rusty pollen. I picked it up and opened the little envelope attached to the cellophane. 'Thinking of you. Abra X.' I felt bad that the sight of my kind, concerned friend's name filled me with another dragging sensation of gloom as I shuffled back inside. Oh well. I'd never had Sam down as a tiger-lily kind of a guy anyway.

*

Sam sat by the window in Bluebell's Diner, staring into a heart-attack milkshake. This was his second trip to the area in two days – he'd visited the cottage despite the lack of response to his messages the day before but the door had remained unanswered. He intended to try again today but the sight of Nick's car outside the house sent him back to the high street, and so, here he was, contemplating a concoction of peanut butter and chocolate ice cream and wondering what to do. She'd obviously let Nick in, he thought. What does that mean?

"It doesn't necessarily mean anything," said Betty, who'd been calling frequently to make sure he didn't bottle out.

"Maybe they've patched things up," said Sam, taking a sip of the thick mud in front of him.

"Honey, that relationship is beyond the point of no return. When did you go over?"

"About two and a half hours and a bacon sandwich ago."

"Oh, she'll have kicked him out ages ago."

"Saw it in your crystal ball, did you?"

"As a matter of fact, I used runes," said Betty sarcastically. "Look, I happen to know that Sylvie likes you and I didn't have to do any divining to work that out, she as good as told me. So go. Go now. Are you going?"

"Yes, your Majesty."

"Love and light!" And with that, she hung up. Sam immediately rang the hallowed number he'd been calling more times than he cared to admit. He was slightly startled when his call was answered.

"Sam! I'm so sorry, I've just picked up all of your messages." Sam felt a twinge of embarrassment. *All* of his messages… "I went a bit underground for a couple of days."

"Completely understandable," said Sam. "Are you all right?"

"I've just… well, I've just split up with Nick. Sam? Are you still there?" I felt strange, it was the first time I'd said the words. It was real. Sam thought he was going to burst.

"Yes. Yes, I'm still here. That's… good?" He desperately wanted to say he was down the road right now, champing at the bit to come over, but thought better of it. He didn't want to rush things. Not that he intended to rush things, but…

"Yes, it's good," I laughed. I desperately wanted to tell him to come over but didn't want him to think I was inviting him round on a rebound impulse. This couldn't be rushed. Not that I wanted to rush things, but…

"I'm so glad," he said, piercing my stream of consciousness. "You made the right decision, if you don't mind me saying. Look, I'm just up the road… "

"Come over."

Sam stayed on the line as he left the diner and walked to my house. But something stopped him in his tracks. He'd gone silent.

"Sam?" I'd obviously talked too much. Great start.

"Hang on." His voice sounded different.

"Are you OK?"

"When did you say Nick left, Sylvie?"

"Couple of hours ago?"

"Well, he's still here," Sam said quietly. "His car's still in your street. He's just sitting there. I can see the back of his head."

"Oh God."

"I don't like the look of it."

"Shit. I hope he hasn't died. He might have overdosed." That had increasingly become the first place my mind went to. It was never out of the question but it was never the case. The man was lucky, I gave him that: heroin consumption in itself aside, how he managed to get home in one piece while off his face was always a wonder to me. His guardian angel must have been the best in the business. But what the hell was he doing? I felt like I was in a movie. Or rather, I wished I was in a movie, and that any moment now someone would say, "Cut!" and I could relax and forget all the scenes I'd just played out, all the lines that had crept under my skin. They wouldn't mean anything to me any more. Someone might even bring me a cup of tea and sort out my hair and make-up.

"Would he really do that in his car? He's kind of on show," said Sam.

"God, he's gone mad. If he sees you he'll do his nut. Not that it matters to me what he thinks," I added quickly. "It's just I don't know what he's capable of."

"Probably not much. But no, you're right. We have to be careful." Any sane person would have suggested calling the police, but, as Les had attested, the police don't tend to take insane pop stars very seriously. They think mania is par for the course, not to mention entertaining. After a caution and a bit of autograph-signing, they let them roam free like chimps in a safari park, at liberty to clamber all over your car, shit on the roof and rip off your wing mirrors before being cute and demanding a bun.

We negotiated the best way of getting Sam in undetected (round the back, through the garden gate and via the kitchen door), and he was soon sitting with me on the sofa, drinking brandy and listening to the whole disturbing story, blow by blow.

I stopped talking when I noticed Nick's mug, still brimming with now-cold tea. Something about it flooded me with dread; evidence that he had been there just a few hours earlier, warming his hands on it. Something of him still seemed to be in the room and it was as if my words were crystallising into 3-D; it was no longer a story. Sam, noticing, quietly took the cup to the kitchen. By the time I had told him everything we were both drained, alternately squeezing drops of Rescue Remedy from the pipette straight onto our tongues, huddling together on the sofa.

Sam was taking great care over his every move, but he hugged me very gently. It was if we'd been made to fit together like two jigsaw pieces. I never wanted to move again.

"What do we do about Nick?" I said eventually, wishing I could just forget everything and drift off on Cloud Sam. "Maybe I should go upstairs and see if I can see him from the window."

"I'll come with you," said Sam, getting up and smoothing down his jumper. I smiled at him and mounted the stairs, listening to his footsteps follow mine. I was only distracted by a sudden horror at the thought of Sam seeing my bedroom until I remembered that I'd done a proper Mary Poppins on it – and myself – earlier that day. Staying close to each other, we moved towards the window.

"There he is," I whispered. "Why is he doing this? The one time he's as attentive as a guard-dog is after I've told him where to go... And why am I whispering?"

"I don't know," Sam whispered back. "I imagine Nick's half-deaf anyway, most musicians of his age are. Not that I'm saying he's old. I mean, you know, over forty."

I laughed, before looking back at my ex, my smile dissolving. Nick was wearing dark glasses and it was impossible to tell where he was looking if his eyes were even open. We both agreed Betty should be called. She was already waiting for a call from Sam with an update. She wasn't expecting this.

"Have you tried ringing him?" Betty suggested after much gasping and swearing.

"Sylvie isn't ringing him," said Sam firmly. "I don't think it would work if I rang him. I elect you, Betty. We can watch what happens from here."

And that's what we did. He might not pick up, but surely he'd move, or check if it was me saying I'd come to my senses and wanted him back. (Or rather, taken leave of my senses and wanted him back.)

"He's not answering," barked Betty down the line. "Did he even look at his phone?"

"Didn't move," said Sam.

"OK. I'm coming over." I felt happier when I knew Betty was on her way. She understood what Nick was going through, she knew him better than anybody and wasn't about to take any shit. Plus maybe she'd recognise what had happened to him. No that I really wanted to know. I just wanted him gone.

By the time Betty arrived, we were stiff from holding our breath and contorting ourselves into the space by the window where we were least likely to be spotted. The familiar sight of Betty's copper hair, clashing violently with her fuchsia wrap, broke our tension. She looked like a mad, matriarchal super-heroine.

She walked straight up to Nick's car, looking in through the window. She rapped on the windscreen. Finally she yelled through the tiny crack at the top of the window and Nick started into life as if he'd been given an electric shock. At least he wasn't dead. The thought that he might overdose right on my doorstep just to spite me hadn't entirely left my mind until now.

We watched Betty's arms flailing and occasionally reaching through the now open window to jab at Nick, who was, again, largely motionless after the initial jerk of movement. But then he gripped the wheel and sped away, leaving her in the middle of the street, shouting after him. Curtain-twitchers appeared at windows. A man with a chihuahua scurried past looking at his feet, clearly praying he could get past Betty unharmed as she finally walked towards the house, muttering curses.

"He was asleep. He's like a fucking narcoleptic," she grumbled, settling in her usual spot on the sofa.

"That was it? He'd just dropped off? I thought he was turning into some kind of stalker."

"Or that he'd carked it," added Sam. Betty laughed bitterly.

"He wasn't moving!" I protested, wedging myself between the pair of them. "What were we supposed to think?"

"I don't blame you for thinking anything. But no, he'd just blacked out for a bit, it happens when he's really stressed. His system goes into overdrive and he shuts down like an old PC. I had a go at him for freaking you out though."

Sam shook his head. "Something about this doesn't sit right."

"What do you mean?" enquired Betty. She liked being the 'sorter-outer' and didn't appreciate being questioned.

"Don't know."

"Helpful."

"I just don't believe he could have fallen asleep after what happened."

"I told you, it's like narcolepsy. It's happened before. An upset like that could easily send him off."

"I think he was pretending," said Sam. Betty looked at him sharply. "I'm sorry, Sylvie, I don't want to scare you. I just think there's no harm in being careful. Nick's hard to read. And you can't apply rational explanations to someone who behaves irrationally."

"He behaves rationally for a heroin user," countered Betty. "This is textbook stuff."

A message buzzed on my phone. "Nick." I whispered. My audience leaned in to look. 'To my bride-to-be. I'll see you tomorrow.' I felt cold. I stared at the text for a few moments. "Maybe it's from the other day and it came through late?"

Betty grabbed the phone and checked. The text had only just been sent. It vibrated again. 'Sylvie.' That was it. And then it vibrated again. 'Be at my place for 8am, I have something for you.'

"8am? God, he really has lost it," concluded Betty. "If I'm honest, I thought it was odd that Nick accepted the decision without a fight. I know this is confusing but you must know his feelings for you run very deeply," she said, turning to me. "It wouldn't surprise me if he just hasn't accepted it at all. You know what the guys in the band are like. If they don't get their way, they're not the kind of people to shrug and move on. Nick wouldn't make a scene like Gomez, but that doesn't mean he isn't the same deep down in that respect."

"You mean, his way of coping with the split is by pretending it isn't happening, just because it's not what he wants?" asked Sam.

"If that text is anything to go by," said Betty, twisting her mouth as she thought about it. "It's like he's rewriting history to try and fix it." She turned to me again. "How clear were you that it was over?"

"Very."

"What's this?" Betty grabbed my left hand and wiggled my ring finger, still weighed down by Nick's diamond. "That's got to go."

I looked at it. I'd become so used to it I'd forgotten to yank it off and hand it back, which was the sort of thing I'd previously fantasised about in darker moments. I inwardly kicked myself for missing the opportunity.

"That's if you're sure?" Betty added. "No sub-conscious urges to hang on to him that made you want to keep the ring, I take it?"

"No! God, no… " Off it came, twisted off slowly with the aid of a dab of Vaseline. Betty grabbed it before I had time to think.

"I'll send it to him in a Jiffy bag tomorrow."

"No, Betty! It's incredibly valuable."

She ignored me, sticking the ring inside the zip-up pocket in her handbag as I stole a final glimpse of it. "This should make the point. As long as you're still wearing it, he'll think there's hope. Getting that ring back in the post in a recycled Jiffy bag should bring it home. And in the meantime, don't speak to him, don't answer the phone to him, nothing. I've had stalkers before, it's no joke," she said, with a tinge of pride.

"So he is turning into a stalker?" I shrank into my seat.

"He's got potential," said Betty. "Sitting outside your flat, sending texts like that… Anyway, I'll make some tea," she said, giving my hand with the now naked, indented ring-finger a little pat before freeing herself from the squashy clutches of the sofa. She smiled, looking briefly over at Sam and me, my hand tucked inside his. At least that looked like it was heading in the right direction, just as Betty had prophesied.

"Would you stay tonight?" I asked.

"Which one of us are you talking to?" asked Betty over the rising steam of the kettle. She noticed Sam flush a little.

"Both of you. If you're OK with it? I wouldn't normally ask but… "

"Of course," said Sam.

"I can sleep on the sofa," offered Betty.

"No, I will," said Sam. "What if Nick comes back? It'll be safer if I'm down here."

"That's exactly why *I* should sleep down here. If he comes back I can confront him, it's better that way." I cringed at the idea of Nick coming back at all, but they were right, we couldn't rule anything out.

"Where should I go then?" asked Sam carefully.

"There's a spare room next to mine," I said, accepting a cup of tea and a Bourbon from Betty. "Oh shit."

"You don't like Bourbons?"

"I've just remembered Nick's got a key. I'll have to double-bolt everything from now on. God, this is insane. "

Sam got up. "I'll do the front door now." Betty turned to me as he headed out to the hall.

"You and Sam… !" she mouthed, eyes bulging with barely contained delight.

"Calm down," I mouthed back. Betty sat back down with her

mug – she'd chosen camomile tea in a bid to stay calm. It was not working. She was doing all she could not to explode.

The phone buzzed again.

"I'll take care of it," said Betty, seizing the phone and shoving it into her bag.

"Aren't you going to look at it?" asked Sam. Betty shook her voluminous head. "We can't be tossed up and down on the choppy seas of Nick's mad texts. It's not going to help anything."

"You think it's going to be another mad one?" I asked.

"You think it isn't? Let him get this out of his system. You can't respond anyway. He did all sorts of weird things before he went into rehab last time. You can't engage with it." Betty zipped her bag and got up to switch on the lamps. The phone buzzed from inside the carpet-bag again. Betty briefly caught Sam's eye.

"Betty?" I ventured, leaning towards the bag. "Maybe I should take a look."

"It's just going to be silly, freaky texts!" barked Betty, spraying the coffee table with crumbs. "No point in looking at them, it'll only unsettle you. All of this will have died down by tomorrow and he'll have come to his senses. If not, I'll cart him to the Priory myself. But in the meantime," she said, lifting her gaze piously, "we mustn't give his negativity any energy. I love him but he's toxic." And with that, she posted another biscuit into her mouth.

The landline jangled and I thought I was going to have a heart attack. Betty waved a hand, indicating we should leave it. But the answerphone kicked into action and now Nick couldn't be ignored. For better or worse he had an audience and Betty couldn't censor him. What followed was a silence, followed by the clearing of a throat.

"Someone's called by mistake," suggested Betty hopefully.

"It's Nick," the disembodied voice said after a moment of dead air. Betty rolled her eyes. "Sylvie? Can you hear me? It's Nick," he repeated. He left a pause as if waiting for an answer before continuing in broken sentences as if he was talking to himself. "I need to talk to you. I need to… I can't… Just… Please."

I looked at Betty, who was staring resolutely at the answering machine, willing it to break.

"I can't accept it, Sylvie. We have to talk right *now*." It was startling to hear him raise his voice. It felt strange, spooky. "OK, I know you're there. I'm coming over."

Betty flew to the phone and clicked the speaker-phone button before he disconnected. "No, you are not!" she yelled.

"Betty? Oh, for fuck's sake… "

"I am looking after the place as Sylvie has gone away, so I'd appreciate it if you didn't come round because *I* don't want to see you."

"Gone where? I have to see her. Is she with someone else? Fucking… Betty, you have to tell me where she is. We need to fix this." Agitation was rising in his voice. I didn't know whether I should be listening to any of this or not, but I had no choice, I was riveted.

"I'm not telling you anything. It's got fuck all to do with you now. She gave you an opportunity to fix things and you bloody well ballsed it up."

"So she is with someone? Not that bastard roadie? It's Sam, isn't it? My Sylvie – *my* Sylvie – with that… *Sam*," he hissed. "I'm going to kill him." Betty turned to Sam, who now looked slightly pale, and shook her head reassuringly. "The cunt's poisoned her against me."

"I don't think he had to, Nick. Look, I don't know what's going on, but you have to stop bothering Sylvie. You've had your chance. And stop bloody texting – you've been texting every five minutes, it's really very boring."

"Aha! How do you know I've been texting?"

"Well… she left her phone behind, didn't she? I'm sick of hearing it buzz every time you get it in your head that you can somehow win her back with a pathetic text. If you don't stop acting like this you know what's going to happen, don't you?"

"You can't tell me how to behave."

"What's going to happen?" asked Betty in a primary school-teacher voice.

"Betty… "

"PRIORY," she snapped.

"I don't need rehab. I need to sort this out. This is between Sylvie and me and that Sam, who I'm going to have to kill."

"PRIORY!" repeated Betty, more forcefully this time. Shouting single well-chosen words was Betty's favourite way of verbally beating people into submission. "You're being mad. You just can't tell that you're being mad because, sadly, that's one of the symptoms of being mad. Get some sleep."

"I'm not mad," protested Nick. "I just want Sylvie back."

"Ah, you've finally realised what you had now it's too late. Mazel tov."

"I'll do whatever it takes."

"That's bollocks and you know it," said Betty. "And what's all this 'bride to be', 'see you tomorrow', 'pretend everything's fine' nonsense? You're delusional."

I listened to the shamed silence at the end of the phone. It was what Nick needed to hear and it was as well that it was coming from someone else. Emotions would have taken over otherwise. While Nick might not have given much away, underneath that saturnine exterior he was all about extremes. Romance became obsession. All-consuming love or resentment would seethe inside him; there was no middle ground. I knew he loved me, but knowing wasn't enough when he seemed incapable of showing me in the most basic of ways up to now. He'd devalued everything we had. Now he wanted it all back, but I had nothing left for him. It was sad, but it was also incredibly stupid. He just couldn't see why I'd had enough.

Nick was beaten, for now. "Tell Sylvie I called… and that I love her… and tell her no one will ever love her as much as— "

"Bye then!" interrupted Betty, disconnecting the call before any more of his platitudes could seep towards me. "No one will ever love her as much as me." He hadn't even managed to get the full sentence out but it still had the ring of a threat, a curse. How he could have believed it himself was beyond me. On the other hand, I didn't have much hope if it was true.

As soon as she'd hung up, Betty started spritzing my aura with her neroli and rose spray, blended by her own hand for occasions such as these. It got quite a bit of action around Concierge.

"Don't let it get under your skin," she soothed, spraying until my hair flattened to my head before giving Sam a spritz. "He's in shock. He's always been dreadful at processing his feelings, let alone when he's on the old gear, believe you me. He'll stop this soon enough if he doesn't want to go to the Priory. And trust me, he doesn't. The merest mention of twelve-step programmes turns him into a wreck. Tomorrow will be different, I promise."

Nobody believed her. In fact she didn't even believe herself. She sprayed herself for good measure and rummaged in her bag again. She was sure there was a hip-flask of something comforting in there somewhere. Preparation for the night ahead.

An unfamiliar sense of tranquility emanated from Concierge HQ on Friday morning. There was no shouting, no smashing of breakables. But Les was definitely in – his elegant green Mercedes was outside and… was that whistling?

Hesitant as ever, Louis tapped on Les's door with the handle of his tailoring scissors.

"Come!"

Louis opened the door a crack and looked through, regarding the scene in front of him with cautious wonder. Les was at his desk with his feet up, hands behind his bullet head. He looked different without the grooves of worry etched across his brow, and the skin on his face looked as if it didn't know what to do now it was robbed of its usual job – crumpling itself up with stress.

"Yes?" prompted Les.

"I wondered if you'd like a coffee?"

"I can do better than that." Les gestured to the chair on the other side of the desk for Louis to sit on and poured two whiskies, handing one over.

"Um… "

"What? Yes, I know, I don't have ice. What do you think this is, The Savoy?"

"No, I mean… isn't it a bit early?"

"Time is a liquid concept, my friend," said Les. "No pun intended. Ha!" Louis jumped slightly at the blast of laughter from the other side of the desk, before taking a tiny sip. The last thing he had tasted was a bowl of Raisin Bran and some coffee, but the trickles of alcohol were abrasively cleansing his palate.

"So…"

"It's very… calm down here," said Louis, taking a gulp for courage.

Les frowned. "Is that unusual?"

"Well, yes."

"You came down to see what was up then, you nosey old fruit?" Louis shrank a little and held the glass in front of himself like a shield. Les let forth another roar of laughter. "Oh, I may as well tell you the good news – although you'll be one of the first to know so you've got to keep it under your, you know, Jewish cap thing."

"Kippa?" offered Louis, touching the skullcap that covered his wispy pate lightly with one nervous finger.

"That's the fella." Les settled back into his chair and lit a small cigar, continuing Concierge's general flagrant disregard for smoking bans. It was clearly very good news. Louis tried not to cough in case Les thought he was trying to hint.

"To cut a long story short, and after a lot of phone calls and negotiations… Ta-dada-DAH! Kurt Christmas from the Idiots is going to be our new lead singer and guitarist." He held up a publicity shot of a hefty man in a checkered suit and sunglasses. Louis peered at the picture through his spectacles.

"Kurt Christmas?"

"From the Idiots. Huge band. You wouldn't know him."

"Au contraire. I made that suit," countered Louis, pleased that for once he knew what Les was talking about.

"No!"

"Have you… met him?"

"Just spoken to his management. What? Don't tell me he's

another maniac. The number of lunatics that have passed through this band… " Les poured more whiskey.

"Well, he used to have a bit of a thing for, you know, *the drugs*," Louis added confidentially. "But he's been clean for years. He just has a few… erm… nervous tics. A hangover from his coke-taking days, but apparently the fans love it, so he makes the most of it. Made measuring his inside leg a bit of a nightmare though. I ended up with two black eyes."

"He must be doing something right. The Idiots are massive," said Les. "We're lucky to have secured him for the tour. And get this: he doesn't even need to rehearse. His manager says he's learning the set and he'll see us at sound-check. Put the wind up me at first, but that's how he works, and who am I to argue with the mighty Kurt? Means I don't have to pay him for rehearsals too." He puffed on his cigar.

"Have the others heard the… er… happy news yet?" asked Louis, noticing with dismay that his glass had been topped up without him realising. He was doing so well with it and now he had to work his way through another one. He was starting to feel it.

"Listen to you getting all involved! No, I only sealed the deal this morning and it's still just after 11am, the little darlings will still be in the land of Nod," winked Les.

"That's it then? No more Gomez? Won't the fans be disappointed? Christmas is nothing like Gomez." Louis might have kept himself to himself but he was nothing if not observant. Gomez was obnoxious and silly but he and Kurt were like multi-coloured chalk and some highly unpredictable cheese.

Les smiled. "We haven't seen the last of Gomez. I have a plan, Louis. All will be revealed soon. Kurt Christmas is not the only surprise Concierge will be getting today."

Louis looked at him expectantly.

"No. I'm not telling you any more. How do I know you're not going to go straight to *The Sun*? Go on, fuck off, some of us have got work to do," said Les. "Any more rock stars coming to have their trousers taken in? Or rather let out? I suppose that would be more appropriate these days… With the exception of our Nick, anyway. Skinny bastard."

"GI diet?" asked Louis innocently. He'd read about it in a magazine one of his customers had left behind and thought he'd try it out as a suggestion. It sounded as stupid as he thought it would.

"Ha… no."

"Atkins?"

"Have you seen *Trainspotting*?"

"Is it a documentary?"

"Well… No, look, never mind. He's just under a lot of stress," said Les. "But we love him. He's my favourite sociopath, and I've met a few. Anyway, you were saying? Who else is beating a path to your door that I should know about?"

"No rock stars that I can think of," said Louis, putting his glass back on Les's desk and stumbling slightly on his way to the door. "Clarence Lillywhite-Barnet is coming in later though."

"The bloke who flounces around buggering up people's houses for them on TV? I know the one. What's he having done, dare I ask?"

"I'm embroidering a waistcoat for him," said Louis, feeling slightly embarrassed. Les gave a derisory hoot of laughter. "In fact, I'd better go and make that coffee. God knows how it'll end up if I don't. I'm not used to drinking this early in the day."

"What are you talking about?" guffawed Les. "He'll love it! It'll be awful! The drunker the better!" And with another gale of laughter he regally waved him away.

Les picked up his phone and decided who to call first. Johnson would be up by now, Abra definitely. Nick, he would leave until last. But then he changed his mind. Talking to them on the phone was a palaver. They asked too many questions. It was best to get them all together first.

And so another of his distinctly threatening round robin texts was sent, inviting them all to the Coach and Horses in Soho for lunch, on him. They might have all been relatively well-heeled but none of them could resist being taken for lunch, it made them feel even more important. The only band-member who wasn't bothered about being invited out for meals was Nick. He'd rather he didn't have to leave the house for something as insignificant as eating.

Concierge severally turned up at the Coach and Horses for 2pm, causing drinkers to pause and gawp as they always did at these exotic creatures. There was Abra, strutting in in her Betty Wright via Neptune garb, and Johnson, who roared up on his motorbike and strode in like an ageing cowboy. Eventually even Nick, looking haunted and pale in a black hooded jacket, dragged himself in. He was a little late, but he was there, which Les had prepared himself not to expect. He slowly drifted over and placed a bony hand on Les's shoulder.

"Fuck me, don't sneak up on me like that! I thought it was the Ghost of Christmas bleeding Future."

"Which one's he?"

"Which one do you think, Nick? The jolly one who looks like Santa? Christ… " Les sipped his pint grimly.

"Does that make you Scrooge?" said Abra.

"My sides," dead-panned Les. "Anyway, sod Dickens. What are you having to drink?"

"Sloe gin please."

"Sloe gin? We're still in *A Christmas Carol.* Give me strength."

"They have it," said Nick, sitting down and resting his head on the table, hands limply hanging down by his sides. Johnson and Abra looked at each other.

"Sloe gin," sighed Les as he made his way to the bar and spent the next five minutes trying to explain to the teenage barmaid what sloe gin was while she looked at him blankly.

Johnson patted Nick on the back. "You all right, man?"

"Haven't slept."

"Something happened?" asked Johnson. "Are you and Sylvie… you know, OK?" Abra kicked Johnson under the table. Nick lifted his head and shook it slowly with half-closed eyes, before letting it drop back on the wooden table with a thud, which looked like it might have hurt. He didn't seem to notice if it did. "We split up."

Both Abra and Johnson simultaneously became fountains of comforting clichés and consoling noises, awkwardly patting the taciturn form between them.

"One sloe gin." Les banged the glass in front of Nick and sat back down. "What's going on?"

"Sylvie and Nick – it's over," whispered Abra.

"Shit," said Les. "If there's anything I can do… "

"No," said Nick through a mouthful of his own hair. "I'm trying everything and it's just making it worse. I think I'm losing my mind."

"Erm… oh. Oh dear." Les was never very good at times of trouble when it came to romance. Sorting out band crises he could do. When it came to affairs of the heart, he was useless, not least because he viewed such things as a total waste of time.

"Sorry, Les, you wanted to tell us something," said Nick, pushing his hair out of his face.

"Ah… yes, I did. And it's good news. Might even take your mind off Sylvie for a bit." Abra pulled a face. How crap was he?

"Go on," said Nick blackly.

"Two things. One: we have a new lead singer for the tour. Kurt Christmas. He's raring to go and he's sure to pull in a whole new fanbase for us."

"Not Jerky Kurt?" said Johnson. "The one with the tics?"

"Is he the one who changed his name so he could have the same initials as Kentucky Fried Chicken?" asked Nick.

"Middle name Frederick," confirmed Les wearily. "Yeah. Great sense of humour."

"I'm sure he'll be… really good." Abra had heard about Kurt

but she was keen to be constructive, if only to prevent Les from bursting a blood vessel.

"That's the end of Gomez, then?" said Johnson, rather sadly. Gomez and Johnson's bromance was reminiscent of *Whatever Happened To Baby Jane?* but they were still the closest in the group. His rage at his former band-mate's apparent betrayal had softened. He missed being Gomez's wing-man.

Les grinned and took a mouthful of his pint. This couldn't be rushed. "Far from it. I've agreed to give him and that mad-woman their first proper gig as Aviary."

"Oh?"

He took a deep breath and delivered the punch. "Supporting us on the tour."

"You what?"

"Nick, you reacted! I did not see that coming," said Les.

"But why?" cried Johnson. "Fans are going to wonder why he's there as the support but not as the main act. I don't exactly understand it myself."

Les smiled enigmatically. "Think about it. Gomez has an ego the size of Jupiter. He thinks he's indispensable, but as soon as he sees we've managed to get a heavyweight star to fill his shoes, and that he'll just be relegated to the support slot with this Aviary farce – which, I wager, will be laughed off the stage from the first night – he'll be back in the Concierge fold before you can say... before you can say... oh, I don't know... "

"Antidisestablishmentarianism," suggested Abra.

"Floccinaucinihilipilification," offered Nick.

"Ooh, good one."

"Don't patronise me, Johnson."

"Aaaanyway," Les continued. "That's the plan. I spoke to them about it and it's all sorted. Well, I spoke to Carly. Gomez was having one of those Gary Rufus pedicures at the time and couldn't come to the phone."

"Gary Rufus?"

"He's a footballer," explained Johnson.

"It's Garra rufa," corrected Abra. "Little fish nibbling your feet."

"Whatever." Les was getting impatient. "What do you think? Not that it matters what you think because it's all been arranged anyway. But still. What do you think?"

The three band-mates looked at each other.

"It could work," said Johnson.

Abra frowned. "What about Kurt? Do we just ditch him as soon as Gomez decides he wants in again?" Abra was quite looking forward to life in Concierge without Gomez.

Les shook his head. "He knows everything. He's in on it. It's no skin off his nose. I'm paying him a block payment for the whole tour plus he gets a shed-load of publicity on the back of the whole Gomez circus. It's win-win. Nick? Any more words for us on this? Apart from floccynocky-something or other? Something that actually means something?"

"Floccinaucinihilipilification does mean something," said Nick. "It's the habit of estimating something as worthless."

"Oh, it would be, wouldn't it? Fuck it. Let's eat. I'm having a pie."

"Just as well, that's all they do – apart from sausage rolls, which are pretty much pies in their own way," Johnson mumbled. He'd been nibbling on a pricey packet of Stilton-flavoured crisps to keep himself going.

Nick rose creakily. Every bit of him ached. "I'm not hungry," he yawned. "I have to go, if that's everything?"

"But we were going to have a band lunch to celebrate my dastardly plan," protested Les. "Besides, you look like you could do with a square meal."

"Stuff to do." He pulled his hood back over his head.

"What stuff? I know all your stuff," complained Les. This time it was his turn to be kicked under the table by Johnson.

"Not all of it," said Nick, stalking out.

"Sylvie stuff," said Abra after he'd gone. "Obviously."

"So he's been dumped?"

Johnson nodded. "I'm worried about him, Les."

"Just as long as he doesn't go round trying to sack any more valuable crew-members, they don't grow on fucking trees," said Les. "Maybe he'll try to sack Sylvie. I'm not having that. She's got to help with the stage designs for the tour. Aviary in particular have some pretty complex ideas."

Abra whacked his arm with a menu. "This isn't a joke, Les. He's already on smack which, in case it hadn't occurred to you, needs sorting."

"He's not on it today, I can tell. Anyway, it's never a problem on tour," insisted Les. "It's only when he's bored and has nothing to do. Almost every band has a heroin addict, anyway, it's practically mandatory."

"We need to take this seriously," persisted Abra.

"She's right," said Johnson. "He's just been given the boot by the woman he loves. He's diving straight into the brown stuff. And you know what'll happen next, don't you? He's going to become fucking hard to play with. And unreliable. And a right downer on the road."

"And we're also worried about him as he's our friend," added Abra pointedly. "What if he does something stupid?"

Les rubbed his chin thoughtfully. And then he opened his mouth to speak.

"Steak and ale, please!" he bellowed to the bar.

Abra rolled her big fluttery eyes.

"Sorry. Ladies first."

"No, Les… I… "

"Look, you're concerned about Nick and that's understandable. But, you know, he's weird. And sometimes he's proper weird. You'll get used to it."

"Johnson's concerned too and he's been around Nick since day one." Johnson nodded. Although if he was honest, he too was now mostly thinking about pie.

"What happened the last time he started, you know, having problems?" Abra asked.

"Well, it was after the first split," explained Les. "He went kind of mad, and then he went to rehab and then he got clean. That's the short version of the story. I'm sure Betty can fill you in on the gruesome details."

"The common denominator seems to be splitting up. Bands splitting up, relationships splitting up... " added Johnson.

"Oh, he just needs to man up. That's life, mate," huffed Les. "Get on with it."

Abra didn't look convinced.

"I mean, get on with it as in order a pie. They're going to bring them all together so I'm waiting for you to make a freaking decision."

"I'll have the same as you, Les," said Johnson, relieved he was now officially allowed to think about eating and not Nick.

"Fine, me too," said Abra glumly.

"Oh, come on, Abra," urged Les. "I'd been hoping you two might have been a bit more excited about the tour with Kurt. Typical Nick for putting a dampener on things."

"Les!"

"Well... "

"He's got problems."

"You don't say," said Les. "'Oh, I've tried everything'... Really? Everything except trying to get clean."

Abra thought for a moment, tapping the cutlery with her tiger-striped fingernails. "When you said, 'he went a bit mad', what exactly did that entail?"

"Oh," Les sighed. "I don't know... he went into this strange state of apathy – I mean, more so than usual – and then he became kind of delusional. First he started doing interviews, which was unusual for him anyway, but every time the journalist asked him a question the only answer he ever gave was 'Willie Nelson'."

"Oh yeah!" said Johnson. "It was like, 'Why did you split up?'

'Willie Nelson.' 'What are you going to do next?' 'Willie Nelson'. 'What's your favourite restaurant?'— "

"'Willie Nelson', yes, I think I understand," interrupted Abra. "What else?"

"Then, he used to turn up to Johnson's rehearsal room as if they'd organised a get-together, but it would be, like, three months since they'd last spoken. He'd ring me in the middle of the night and rage at me for trying to exclude him from band meetings long after we'd all gone our separate ways."

Johnson nodded again, solemnly. "One night," he said, leaning in, his voice low as if he was telling a ghost story, "he came to my studio, convinced Concierge were in there without him – we weren't, of course, we'd broken up ages before. I'd rented the space to a local band for the day. They were rehearsing and couldn't hear him ringing the intercom, so he drove his car into the door and smashed it open. Cost me a bloody fortune."

"God... "

"He'd been speed-balling," said Les. "It was soon after that that the nice men in white coats came along."

"You don't think... " started Abra.

"What?"

"Well, that he's going to go down a similar route again? With Sylvie, I mean?"

"Shit, I hadn't thought about that," said Johnson.

"How could you not, knowing he's done all that before?"

"Pies," chirped the barmaid shrilly, appearing from nowhere and slapping plates down in front of them.

"JESUS," shrieked Les. "Frightened the shit out of me. Anyway, I'm sick of talking about Nick, all those stories give me the heebie-jeebies. He can take care of himself."

"And what about Sylvie?" said Abra.

"I'd imagine Sam's taking good care of her, isn't that the latest?" Les said, stabbing at the crust with his fork.

"Really?" said Abra. She was put out that, if this was true, she'd had to hear it from Les. "Well, that could make matters worse. Think about it – if you were Nick, and you had that kind of history, what would you be doing right now if your future wife had left you and was now knocking around with someone else? He could be driving his car into her lounge right now."

"Nah. He doesn't want to get put away. And where would he get the energy? Can you honestly say you have met anyone with less get up and go?" Les shook his head. "Just eat your pie."

Nick wasn't going to drive his car into any lounges. He hadn't gone completely off his head. Just enough to put the frighteners on the three people inside that little house in Strawberry Hill.

No one had slept; there was no point in trying. Nick had been ringing through the night, trying the landline to squeeze Betty for information, attempting to break her down the more tired and fractious she became until she just refused to pick up, letting him ramble endlessly into the answer machine. Betty said we should keep these recordings in case there was a police enquiry. By 3am, I'd unplugged the phone.

He was also trying my mobile several times an hour, and he was emailing messages that ranged from heartfelt to venomous to just deranged within minutes of each other. Photographs of the two of us in better times appeared in my inbox, as did some well-chosen YouTube links to emotive music videos and a few typo-riddled Heathcliff-style rants. Everything left me feeling sickened and the more he tried, the stronger my aversion became.

As a teenager, I'd dreamed of having an intense, difficult man fighting to win my love, but the reality was intermittently scary and tiresome. Once, not even that long ago, I'd have loved to have thought Nick would be this anxious to keep me in his life. Now I just wanted him to go away.

By about 8am, the incessant contact stopped for several hours. Betty insisted he had probably fallen asleep, one of the things he did best, and hadn't done anything regrettable. Nothing fatal, anyway. This was proved when, at 3pm, there was a knock on the door; the knock I'd been dreading.

Betty put a finger to her lips. The three of us, who, apart from me, were still in their clothes from the day before (I'd long since graduated to my purple silk pyjamas – silk made most things better, I found), remained motionless. Sam was red-eyed and frazzled, his fingers digging into the soft sides of the armchair.

"It might not be him," whispered Betty hopefully. *Jehovah's Witnesses*, I thought. *Please be Jehovah's Witnesses*. I could see through into the hall without having to get up. And, just as I feared, the messy dark shape of Nick's head was visible through the glass.

"It's him," Betty mouthed.

"God," I groaned. "I can't take much more of this."

Nick put his key into the lock of the bolted door, the familiar 'rrratch' sound turned me cold. After trying in vain to get in, he flipped open the letterbox with a creak. "Open up, Betty."

She waved her arms in an indication that we should get behind the sofa, which we did. I felt like I used to as a child, hiding if someone came to the door when my parents were out; except this felt less exciting and naughty and more nerve-janglingly creepy and I realised my hair was damp with sweat. The idea of hunkering down behind a sofa with Sam would ordinarily be quite appealing, but the circumstances were not ideal. All the same, we shared a private giggle, possibly from sleep-deprived hysteria, as we caught each other's eye.

"Do you come here often?"

Betty leaned over and shushed us harshly, which only made us want to laugh even more. By the time Nick called through the letterbox again, we were almost beside ourselves, cushions stuffed into mouths, tears rolling down cheeks. It was a release of all the tension. Great timing.

Once we had quietened down we heard Betty getting up, with a squeak of the sofa springs. That wiped the smile off our faces.

"She *can't* be answering the door." said Sam.

"Shit, this is like a nightmare."

I peeped around the end of the sofa to see Betty standing by the front door.

"Bet, I know you're in there," said Nick. "I can see your hair."

"Yes, well!" stuttered Betty from the other side of the closed door. "You woke me up, actually."

"It's about 3pm, don't give me that."

"You kept us up all night with your phone calls." Sam and I looked at each other.

"Us? Us? I knew it. Let me in." He plunged his key in with more violence this time and rattled the door in its frame.

"It's bolted, Nick," said Betty calmly.

"Just fucking well let me in, will you? I want to talk."

"I don't feel comfortable about you coming into Sylvie's house while she's away, she wouldn't appreciate it."

"She isn't away! You just said 'us'!" He landed a fist heavily on the door. "Ow... Bugger. Look, I know she's in there."

"We've been through this," sighed Betty. "I think I'm going to have to make some phone calls... "

"Oh, no you don't... "

"... regarding the Priory."

"For Christ's sake."

"You OK?" whispered Sam, touching my shoulder. I could feel he'd been watching my face throughout, monitoring every emotion. I gave him a nervous smile and he put an arm around me.

"Maybe I should talk to him," I murmured.

"What?" This was tantamount to letting the vampire over the threshold.

"Keep it down, Sam, please."

"I mean, do what you feel is best. But really... you can't... "

"What was that?" Nick's voice cut through. "There's a man in there!"

"I think I'd have noticed."

"Betty, I heard a man's voice!" Nick kicked at the door. "If Sam is in there with Sylvie I will not be held accountable for my actions."

"All right! It's him. I admit it." Sam and I stared at each other again. What the hell was she doing?

Nick crumpled a little, as if he'd received a blow to his solar plexus. Finally the words came, hissed out in a furious tangle that no one could decipher. I closed my eyes as I heard Nick's boot doing battle with the front door. So far the door was winning.

"I mean, he's here for me," said Betty. "We're... we're having an affair." Sam's eyes widened. Neither of us could deny it was a master-stroke. Betty had bought herself a little more time.

"You must think I'm an idiot," he said eventually, under his breath.

"It's true!" protested Betty. "Sam?" She hurried to the sofa and suddenly her face loomed over ours. Now was Sam's moment. He silently pulled himself to his feet and followed Betty out to the hall. It was the least he could do, Betty thought. It was his fault for raising his voice, after all.

Carefully, Betty opened the front door, ensuring the sliding chain-lock was safely in place, and looked at Nick through the gap. He felt like he was disintegrating but he was attempting to compose himself and was now leaning against the door-frame. Ray-Bans, black overcoat... every inch the elegant pop star. He had to at least look as if he was in control.

"Well, here I am... " Sam reluctantly appeared in the gap. "And it's true, me and Betty are, erm... you know. An item."

Nick took him in for a moment. "Don't B.S me, mate."

"I know it's uncomfortable, Nick," said Betty, her voice rising. "We've been trying to keep it a secret."

"Well, you succeeded," Nick smiled thinly. "Most of us had the impression Sam was after Sylvie."

"Look, this is very embarrassing for all of us," said Sam. "Just… be on your way."

"Be on my way?"

"Yes."

"Kiss her," said Nick. He didn't actually want to see them kiss at all but they'd have to do better than this to get rid of him.

"Nick," said Betty, placing her hands on her hips. "We are not performing seals."

"I'm not so sure."

"Nick!"

"I think you could be."

They were going to have to do this. Betty was rather pleased, although she'd have preferred it if the circumstances might have been a little more relaxed; less of a gunpoint vibe would have been nice. Sam kept repeating the words *do it for Sylvie, do it for Sylvie* in his head.

I was rigid behind the sofa, reminding myself to breathe. Knowing that the door was open even slightly was not comforting. Knowing that Betty was about to kiss Sam was just weird and kind of funny. Maybe it was unfair, but everyone in Camp Concierge saw Betty as a cuddly, bossy matriarch, not the sort of woman who would go round kissing the face off cute younger blokes. Maybe we were all underestimating her.

"Go on, display your love," said Nick, watching Sam and Betty dither. Finally she lunged at him. He closed his eyes quickly in a bid to look more 'in the moment'.

"Happy?" Sam pulled away after an obligatory few seconds.

"No, I am not. Don't ever try and trick me again, either of you. And that was every bit as disgusting as I expected it to be."

"How dare you!"

"Because it was fake, Betty. It was all just part of this pathetic charade to keep me away from Sylvie. Now let me in." And with that, he crashed into the door with all of his strength, superhuman with anger. Sam rushed forwards to block his path and was swiftly head-butted in the face. I heard a body fall against furniture and onto the floor but I didn't dare move. Nick wasn't stupid. He knew if he'd hurt Sam, I'd soon come out of the woodwork.

Blood gushed from Sam's nose, soaking his T-shirt. Nick had actually managed to knock him out. He'd also nearly knocked himself out in the process. After a few stunned seconds, he took a moment to survey his victim. He was fascinated by what he'd just achieved. It was so out of character. Betty shrieked at her brother, partly as a signal to me to escape through the back door, partly from pure fear. She never thought she'd see this side of him again.

The time had come to call the police. I strained to reach Betty's bag but it was just that little bit too far away; I had no choice, I had to stand. I crept around the back of the sofa, trying hard not to look into the hall, hoping against hope that if I didn't look, somehow that would render me invisible too. Steadying myself with one hand, I reached out my free arm and snatched the bag towards me, digging inside for the phone. There were so many pockets, so much paraphernalia, so much maddening noise to try to tune out. But there it was, missed calls racking up on the screen, battery nearly dead.

Nick moved towards Sam slightly, looking at his bloodied face as he woozily started to come round. "Don't!" yelled Betty, dabbing his bleeding nose with her sleeve.

"You're out of your mind," groaned Sam as Betty helped him to his feet, guiding him as quickly as he could comfortably go to the bathroom to bathe his face. But Nick didn't respond. Something else had caught his attention. Soft, hurried whispers coming from the lounge, whispers no one else had heard. Betty was convinced I'd done the sensible thing and left the house via the back. But, despite her best efforts, Nick had found what he was looking for.

22

"Sylvie?" Nick moved slowly into the lounge, as if he was trying to lure out a wild animal. He approached the sofa and peered over the top.

"Stay away from me!" I rose awkwardly, clinging onto a curtain for support. Emotions pulsed through me, clashing against each other – I felt impossibly vulnerable and at the same time absolutely livid. Apart from anything else, he'd freaked me out to the extent I felt I had to hide in my own home because I had no idea what he was going to do next. That was not on.

"What? Were you hiding? From me?" Nick took off his sunglasses and squinted against the light. "I've been trying to— "

"Call me? Yes, I know." I gripped the back of the sofa. It felt good to have something solid between me and Nick. "And I got all of your texts, your emails… "

"You all lied," he said.

"Never mind that, what have you done to Sam?"

Nick opened his laser-beam eyes a little. "He was in my way. Why is he here?"

"You were scaring me. He was looking out for me, same as Betty. I'm allowed friends— "

"He's after more than that."

"What has that got to do with you anymore? We're finished."

"No."

"We are. It wasn't a question." I emerged unsteadily. "Let me pass, I need to see if Sam's— "

"Is that why, then?" asked Nick, his hand locking onto my arm. "So you could be with him?"

"Us splitting up has nothing to do with anyone else."

He pulled me in closer. I stiffened refusing to look into his eyes.

"The police will be here in a minute."

"Police?" he laughed. "Why?"

"You've been harassing me."

"No, I haven't."

"You broke down my door. You assaulted someone. I think that's enough to be going on with."

"Crimes of passion," he breathed, touching his forehead against mine. "I thought you'd be into that, Sylv."

I shook my head, fighting ingrained weaknesses, the easy temptation of an old attachment, his voice, his familiar smell.

"I haven't touched any gear for two days."

"Congratulations. You're simply adorable off it."

"I'm trying… "

"POLICE!" Two chubby uniformed officers stepped through the destroyed door-frame and straight into the living room, their lumpen gait making Nick look strangely graceful.

"We had a call about harassment and a break-in."

"Well, yes, as you can see… "

"There's been a misunderstanding," began Nick suavely.

"There has not, Nick."

"Hang on," said the more rotund of the pair. "It *is* you! I knew it as soon as I walked in and saw that hair! PC Ball, it's an honour to meet you, sir. I'm a huge fan."

"Me too!" said the younger officer, his voice slightly strangulated from excitement. He breathlessly took off his helmet and extended a hand. "PC Davidson. I thought *Tenements of Madness* was a masterpiece. Especially your songs. My Mum's got all your records. I went to my first Concierge concert when I was ten."

"Oh. Er… thanks very much." Nick's red, narrowed eyes flicked from one officer to the other, then back to me.

"I'm sure we can get this sorted out in a jiffy," said Davidson. He whipped out his notebook. "Would you, you know… would you mind signing this?"

Ball winked at me. "Comes to something when even Nick Sinclair can't make a young lady happy." He was being dangerously over-familiar. I wondered whether Nick might like to try that head-butting thing out again. "No offence, of course, I didn't mean like… in the… er— "

"Shut up!" said Davidson through his teeth.

"What started the fight then, eh? Was he spending too much time strumming the old geetar, eh?" Ball added brightly, trying to change the subject.

"I play keyboards," muttered Nick.

"You see," Ball turned to me. "Artists like Nick – I can call you Nick, can't I? – artists like Nick are passionate, some people don't know how to handle it, I suppose. Misunderstood." He smiled at Nick knowingly and raised a little fist of solidarity, as if to say, "I hear you, brother."

This was surreal. It wasn't like it hadn't happened before, but now Concierge had gone beyond its post-split bit-of-a-naff-joke phase, and was now in a post-ironic genuinely-quite-cool-again era, Nick was experiencing embarrassingly royal treatment and even he wasn't entirely comfortable with it. "Officers— "

"No, Nick, I get it. I mean, you couldn't write a song like 'Laser Eraser'— "

"Oh, I love that one," interjected Davidson.

"… without having experienced real emotional turmoil. I guess we can't all express it the way you do, but it really spoke to me."

"I didn't write 'Laser Eraser'," said Nick. They didn't hear.

"I suppose you'll be writing a song about all of this next," chortled Davidson. "Maybe you'll mention us in the lyrics!"

"There's a man bleeding in my bathroom!" I yelled. And I wasn't suggesting it as a possible lyric either. Where were these policemen from? Trumpton? "He did that," I continued. "Mr Sensitive Soul flipping Laser Eraser."

Nick raked his hand through his hair irritably. "I *didn't write* 'Laser Eraser'…" In actual fact, 'Laser Eraser', written by Johnson Large, was a song imagining how the world would be if we all had 'eraser beams' that could shoot from our heads and delete mistakes, wiping the slate clean every time something regrettable happened. This was a superpower Nick would have paid good money for right now.

"Oh dear. Well, we'll have to have a chat with him then, I suppose. Artistic temperament, eh? This way, is it?" asked Ball, as he took his time negotiating his way through the hall, scattering bits of wood and broken ornaments with his feet. "Crimes of passion… "

"Something like that."

"Keep him out!" yelled Betty from behind the bathroom door as she heard the men approach. "He's mad!" The officers looked at Nick reassuringly before continuing to the bathroom.

Nick smiled, approaching me again. "I can't believe you were so scared. It's me. I mean, what did you think I was going to do?"

"I don't know. You've changed, you know you have."

He looked back into the hall and smiled slightly. "Look what you made me do. You're a dangerous girl."

"Nick, that's not funny."

"I've always liked those pyjamas."

"What? Just… don't talk, you're freaking me out again. It's creepy."

"You look like a little bar of Dairy Milk," he purred as I backed into the kitchen. Dairy Milk? He really had lost it.

"Yeah. Purple silk… All that brown hair." He edged closer and stroked some strands of hair out of my face. "Oh Sylvie, what's the matter with you? Let me hold you. It could be the last time."

"No. But I'm glad you seem to get it now."

"I still love you," he persisted. His face was close again, his fingers in my hair, dry lips brushing against mine.

"Don't."

"Kiss me."

"You're just making it harder for both of us." I jerked away from his hands, and folded my arms against him. "I don't even know why you're doing this. Is it because you're so used to getting your own way that you go nuts when you're denied? That isn't love, that's your ego, my friend."

"You love me too, you can't have just stopped," said Nick. "You didn't give back the ring, that has to mean something."

"You can have it back! I'm not even wearing it."

"I don't want it back. God, this is such a waste. When did you become so fucking hard?"

I wasn't rising to this. I hadn't been nearly hard enough. All I wanted now was to go to Sam; it was all I could think about.

"You want to see me suffer." His grip on my arms became harder, fingers digging into my skin. "You're sadistic. You're a sadistic little… "

"Stop. Please Nick, listen to yourself. You're delusional. And lose the victim complex, you're not the only one who's suffered. When will you accept that I don't want this any more?" He closed his eyes and pressed his damp forehead against mine. His whole body lurched a little, as if he was about to collapse, but the grip was still hard, tight.

"God, my head, Sylv."

"What?"

"Well, I nutted him, didn't I? It hurts."

"Oh, you shit, Nick. If you think you're getting any sympathy from me… "

"Right," piped Ball, striding into the lounge. "Gentleman's still woozy. Must have been quite a whack you gave him, Mr Sinclair! The lady will take him to have it looked at. Anyway, erm… I'm afraid we'll have to take you to the station now, sir. PC Davidson will take a statement from the young lady." Nick released me silently after pressing his lips onto my tightly shut mouth. I rubbed my arms where his fingers had been and watched the police officer guide my ex away, cursorily reading him his rights as he was drawn gently towards the squad car.

Watching them leave, I felt as if I could exhale for the first time in ages, even if I knew Nick would only have to sign his autograph on every bit of paper in the police station and reel off a few anecdotes before being sent on his way after a good-humoured caution.

"Erm… Miss?"

I turned to see Davidson hovering expectantly in the lounge with his notepad.

"Oh, yes. Questions. Fire away."

"Yes. Well, to start off with… what's it… you know, what's it like?"

"What's what like?"

"Oh come on. Going out with a pop star! What's it *like*?"

"Troubled 80s heart-throb Nick Sinclair was admitted to a private rehabilitation clinic in north London last night after being arrested for breaking and entering, assault and possession of — "

"I can't listen to any more," said Les, pointing his remote control at the TV and switching over to a *Columbo* re-run.

"Bastards," said Johnson. "So much for police discretion."

"'Troubled'… That's tabloid journalese for 'junkie', isn't it?" asked Abra.

"Funny thing is," began Ange, brushing cigarette ash off her cleavage with a practiced flick. "I know loads of people who are on drugs and they're not troubled at all. They're having a grand old time."

"Looks good on TV though, doesn't he?" offered Pearl.

Ange nodded with enthusiasm. "Oh yes. Quite sexy. Funny how seeing someone on TV does that."

Johnson looked at them contemptuously. "No disrespect, but what the fuck has that got to do with anything?"

"The hair looked good, you have to admit," said Les. If there was one thing he coveted more than Nick's wiry physique it was his hair. Or just any hair. Any hair at all.

As soon as they'd heard the news, everybody in the Concierge camp convened at Les's bachelor pad in Golders Green. His flat was a dated combination of black and chrome 80s luxury and decadent squalor. The state of the bathroom alone indicated that he wasn't used to having visitors.

Apart from the occasional break for bagels at Carmelli's, the all-night bakery nearby, Concierge and co. had been watching the ghastly story crop up on twenty-four-hour news through the night – it was all they could do – watching their friend surrounded by paparazzi on the steps of the police station, looking at his tired, handsome face just as people across the nation would be seeing him as they watched the news, coming in from a night out, eating breakfast with their kids. Abra confirmed that, as of that morning, Nick Sinclair had even become a trending topic on Twitter, not that anyone else in the room understood what that meant.

I, meanwhile, was in Barnes, trying to sleep with little success. Betty had invited both Sam and myself to stay at her house that night – she was insistent that I shouldn't go home until the door-stepping journalists had retreated (and also until the house had been 'cleansed' by some druids she'd met at Badbury Rings). Betty had even rescued Brando and was caring for him until his master was back and capable of looking after another sentient being. She was in full-on Super-Betty mode.

One of the duties she was taking particularly seriously was trying to keep me away from the TV, the newspapers, the radio. The situation was tough enough without being reminded that the whole nation was poring over your personal life. Having Sam around meant Betty could also try to Reiki his nose better – it seemed like the least she could do considering her brother had just busted it. It was such a nice nose as well, although she suspected that once it had healed and the stitches were out, it would have a Romanesque *je ne sais quoi* that would knock his previous schnozzle into a cocked hat. *Way to go, Nick*, thought Betty wryly. *You've made your nemesis even more attractive.*

Les and Johnson had met Betty and I at the police station,

exchanging a few commiserations before we went our separate ways. Les couldn't help but comment on how fragile he thought I was looking. He was concerned for all the wrong reasons.

"This is complicated to say the least," said Les, getting up to make yet more coffee. "Nick will be out of rehab by the end of next week, I'm sure of that. I'll bust him out if I have to. He'll be fine after he's had a few days to think."

"He's not going to get clean in a few days, Les," said Abra.

"Who said he was? He's just going through the motions. Different rules apply to people like him anyway, he can do what he likes."

"What *you* like," muttered Abra.

"I have to say though," continued Les, "His timing has been impeccable – we're getting shit-loads of publicity and we're only weeks away from the tour. From that point of view: bonzer, never loved the man more. Bit of the old 'troubled' caché builds intrigue. I mean, he's a trendy topic on Twitter, for goodness' sake."

"Trend*ing* topic," corrected Ange.

"Whatever. I need him out of there ay-sap and I need Sylvie on form to complete work on costume and stage designs. I've been talking to the production manager and apparently Gomez wants flying rigs."

"Flying rigs?" spluttered Johnson.

"Yes, you know, Aviary, birds, flying… "

"This I have to see." Visions of short, squat Gomez flapping about in a chick costume ping-ponged around Johnson's mind. "And what about *our* stage-set? Or is it all about Gomez again, even though he's not in the band?"

"Space-age," grunted Les, biting into his bagel.

Abra scowled. "You're all heart, you are. That lovely remark about publicity aside, what makes you think Sylvie is going to want to work with Concierge after all of this? She's not going to want to be anywhere near Nick, for a start. He might go mad again, he'll be paranoid about Sylvie and Sam, it's too dodgy."

"Fair point," agreed Pearl, wearily pulling clumped little sleeves of mascara off her eyelashes. "You're dealing with human beings, Les."

"That's a matter of opinion. Look, I'll hire another dresser for Nick or Betty can help out, but beyond that they'll have to sort themselves out. Bunch of adolescents. I warned Nick it was unprofessional when they first got together. Did he listen to me? Did he fuck." He stomped to the window and ripped open the curtains, making everyone cower from the blinding light. "And *now* look where we are."

"In Golders Green," said Johnson.

"Where is Gomez? I thought he'd have been here by now," asked Abra.

Pearl yawned. "On his way."

"With Carly?"

"Afraid so. That's probably why they're late. She's always been high maintenance – she'll have had a freak-out about something. That's what always used to happen."

"So," ventured Johnson. "Is he living with Carly now?"

"He'll be back," said Pearl. "He always comes back. Anyway, this is about his artistic direction, we have to be supportive."

"It's also about him being shit-scared of Carly and what she's capable of," said Les, returning from the kitchen with a sticky tray of mugs.

The intercom buzzed like an angry wasp. Les looked at the video screen. A short, dark curly-haired man and a tall, manic-looking Olive Oyl-type, both of them wearing matching feathery headbands, stared back. "Talk of the devil," smirked Les, releasing the door. "Ladies and gents, I give you Gomez and Cerrrr-azy Carly… "

"Just Carly!" whispered Ange as their footsteps approached. "We don't want her to know we call her that."

"Sure, sure."

Gomez and Carly walked in, regarding their fellow guests

awkwardly. This was the first time Gomez had seen most of them in the flesh since the abduction and he hadn't been forgiven. Carly was, naturally, *persona non grata* and everyone apart from kindly Pearl and who-gives-a-crap Ange avoided eye contact.

"Help yourself to coffee!" blustered Les. "I've made way too many."

"It looks like you've used *all* of your mugs, Les," sniggered Ange. "Did you get a bit carried away?"

"That's just how I roll sometimes."

"That's just how he rolls sometimes," Ange repeated, grinning at Gomez and Carly. "Poor fella ain't slept."

No one made space for them so they leaned uncomfortably against Les's newspaper-strewn dining table. There was so much that needed to be said, so much that was unspoken between Gomez and the rest of the group, but this had, temporarily, been sidelined by the Nick crisis. Still, tension hung in the air like the mugginess before an electric storm.

"Is Nick going to be out in time for the tour?" enquired Gomez. "Not that it would matter that much if he wasn't."

"If you're not going to be constructive then why did you come?" asked Abra.

"Because he told me to with one of his 'on pain of death' text messages," said Gomez, flailing a petulant arm towards Les. "Nick got himself into this mess, he can get himself out. Attention-seeker."

"You just don't like it when the spotlight is on someone else."

"Put a bleeding sock in it," said Les. "And I expected more from you, Ronald Gomez. Is it too much to ask for a bit of fraternity? The point is that Nick will be back, I'm going to make bloody well sure of it. Apart from my obvious concern for the dear man," he said, casting Abra a quick look, "fewer original members means less money. There's only one exception to that rule and that was Henson Bedges. Promoters would have paid us double not to bring that lunatic to their venues. In fact, our fee did go up when

Abra replaced him. We get more gigs now too. Health and safety is no longer a nightmare… "

"And this… Kurt," began Gomez. He looked pained, which pleased Les.

"Kurt is our new singer, I've told you all this. You left, remember? Anyway, I'm doing you a favour before you start beefing on about it; you'll have a captive audience, big venues, good money…"

Gomez pursed his lips. "I don't like him."

"You haven't met him," said Abra.

"Oh, but I have. We met at Glastonbury last year. He called me a… well, I can't remember but it wasn't very nice."

"A 'mulleted knobhead', as I recall," said Les, rather gleefully. "That's just his sense of humour. Anyway, you're not in the band now so it shouldn't be a problem keeping you apart, at the London venue at least. He'll be in Dressing Room One while yours will be waaaay up on one of the upper floors." Les gave Johnson a sly glance. His plan to lure back their star was already working.

"Anyway, we're not here to talk about you, we're here to worry about Nick," added Johnson, glaring at his old friend.

"Useless junkie," sniped Gomez.

"Maybe," said Les. "But he's our useless junkie."

*

When I awoke in Betty's house, for one heart-pounding moment I had no idea where I was. My head throbbed and my jaws hurt after a night of teeth-grinding or jaw-clenching, I wasn't sure which.

Denying my usual urge to switch on the radio, I pulled on the floaty green kimono Betty had left out for me and emerged quietly from the room, peeking in on Sam in the neighbouring bedroom. His face, illuminated by a soft shaft of sunlight and criss-crossed with stitches and white strips of plaster, looked peaceful and almost child-like. He rolled over and I stepped back, nervous of him seeing me. After listening to his hypnotic sleep-breathing for a few more seconds, I pulled the door to and went downstairs, following the alluring scent of coffee that billowed from the hob.

Betty, also in a kimono (violet with cream sprigs), was at the kitchen table nibbling at a piece of toast, her flaming hair temporarily controlled by a fluffy white towel, twisted up into a turban. The kitchen radio being out of bounds as it was, Betty was instead playing vinyl on her record player in the back room, and the sound of Joni Mitchell drifted lightly through the hatch in the wall. "You OK? You could have slept for longer if you'd wanted to."

I smiled at her and poured myself a cup from the pot. "My mind was whirring."

"I'm not surprised. Sam's still sound asleep. Did you look in on him?" There was a whisper of mischief in Betty's question. Well-meaning mischief, but mischief all the same.

"No." I blushed hard. I wished I wasn't such a blusher.

Betty smiled, getting up and giving me a hug. "Either of you sneak in on each other in the night?"

"Betty!"

"Have you two even kissed?"

"I've only just split up with Nick, remember? I don't do overlaps."

"I want to know when I can buy a hat."

"What happened to the one you bought when I got engaged to Nick?"

"I'll level with you, Sylvie, I didn't buy one. Anyway, all in good time. Good morning gentlemen."

"Sorry?"

"Magpies on the front wall. Two for joy."

"I could do with a bit of that," I said, absently stroking the soft sleeve of my kimono.

"You don't have to go back, you know. To the band, I mean," said Betty, pulling a chair out and patting the cushioned seat.

"God, I hadn't even thought about that yet. I can't pull out. Thanks to Les I'm busier than ever and I can't let him down. I need to work anyway."

"Well, you've got enough to think about with the set designs without having to worry about Nick doing all of his buttons up correctly, particularly given his current… unpredictability," said Betty, raising a sculpted brow. I shuddered at the thought of having to go near him again at all. "Les isn't that unapproachable. You just have to make sure he's well-oiled and his Neil Diamond records are on hand. Have a word with him."

"I will. I've got reams of emails from him and Gomez about what they want, it's a bit overwhelming – the beginning of the tour is only next month."

"Well, I'll be there to help."

"But Nick… The thought of seeing his face again makes me feel ill."

"Don't think about that yet," said Betty, pushing a plate towards me. "Eat some toast."

I automatically picked up a slice and guided it into my mouth. I was still a bit in shock.

"Why does Gomez get special treatment then?" asked Betty, changing the subject. "Support bands never have sets designed for them by the headliner's production team."

"It's part of Les's ruse to tempt him back," I explained through a mouthful of toast. "And by that time, there'll have been so much publicity and furore around him leaving and Kurt joining and Aviary and all the rest of it that, by the time he's back in the fold, by Les's estimation at least, it'll be perfect timing to record a new album. Concierge will be 'back on top'," I concluded wearily, quoting Les's latest mantra.

Betty drummed her long nails on the table. "Let me guess. Aviary… Gomez wants feathers?"

"Uh-huh."

"Seriously? I love it. I have to see these emails." Betty put out an expectant hand as I reached over to the worktop for my charging phone. I'd hardly dared look at it since yesterday in case there was anything new on there from Nick, but as I switched it on, all appeared to be quiet on the Sinclair front. Texts beeped one after another from Abra, Pearl, Ange, Johnson, my parents, all of them checking in on me, but nothing from Nick. Then I remembered they'd probably taken his phone at the clinic. Clicking on my emails, I found the list of 'instructions' from Gomez and handed it over to Betty, watching her face as she read it.

"My God… You know he wants to fly onto the stage from the back of the auditorium?"

I laughed. "Yep. The thing is that Les isn't going to want Aviary to upstage Concierge in the set stakes, so I dread to think what he's going to ask for now that Gomez is getting more demanding. It's already going to be space-age. He'll probably want a zero-gravity atmosphere in the venue and a 'moon-landing' entrance for the band."

"Don't give him any ideas," said Betty, scrolling deftly. "Arrrgh, listen to this: 'Feathers must be sourced from St James' Park swans.'"

"I'm getting them from Borovick's in Soho. I'll drape duckweed over them."

Betty was on a roll, gasping with delighted horror as Gomez's email unfolded. "He says they're in the studio now, recording the sound of eggs cracking open. 'This is to be played before the performance commences'… What is he on?" Betty put the phone down at last with a sigh. As she got up to pour herself another cup of coffee, she turned to me. "What's the betting there won't be a load of die-hard Gomez fans in bird outfits on the night?"

"Gomez's fans might be bonkers, and it's a beautiful thought, I grant you, but I can't see them going that far."

"Some of them have had perms just to look like Gomez," Betty reminded me. "I've been around this band a long time, nothing can be ruled out – the fans are way more peculiar than the group.

I'll bet you £20 we'll see at least five feathered friends in the crowd at the warm-up gig alone."

"You're on," I said, shaking her hand. "I wager it'll just be the usual load of fans in Concierge T-shirts and the odd Kurt Christmas fan in a tartan suit wondering whether they're at the right gig."

"Done," said Betty, smiling the smile of someone who knows they've already won.

"That'll be £20 please." D-Day had finally arrived and Betty had not forgotten the wager as we approached Camden's Koko venue for the get-in. It was still only 11am, but after parking the hired van and heading for the stage door, a line of grey and green sleeping bags, initially camouflaged against the dark, rain-lashed bricks of the theatre, became visible.

"Already?" I peered over an armful of suit-bags and looked around. All I could see was what looked like an array of tramps sleeping rough on the pavement.

"Look closer," urged Betty, still with her hand out. I moved towards one of the sleeping bags. Out of the top of it poked a slumbering head encased in a home-made bird head-dress, complete with wilting cardboard beak.

"And here." Betty was not mistaken. At least five out of the eight men camping out in a bid to be the first to glimpse their heroes – specifically Gomez in these cases – were in various states of featheriness. It seemed to be a statement of loyalty.

"Wow," I giggled, stepping over dirty puddles on my way to the stage door. Betty gave a derisive snort, causing two of the men to open a bleary eye briefly before closing it again. Betty and I were not the ones they were waiting to see.

After picking up our laminates and inhaling that familiar

backstage smell – hairspray, sweat, alcohol, dust burning on lightbulbs – we whisked the costumes to the relevant dressing rooms, Betty chatting and singing all the while. After some discussion with Les, she had returned as a wardrobe mistress to ease the pressure and, crucially, ensure I didn't have to go near Nick.

My plan for the day was to get as much done as early as possible, avoid any unwanted encounters and then lurk at the back of the auditorium for the gig itself, a walkie-talkie on hand should I be needed. It had been a while since I'd watched the group from out front and I was intrigued by how it would look and sound, particularly as I'd had more to do with the visual aspect of the show than ever before. I was already tingling with excitement, not least because I hadn't slept much the night before. OK, so I hadn't told Betty yet, but the past three nights had been spent in an impermeable love bubble with Sam. He was perfect. He made me feel perfect. Basically, it was all pretty darn perfect, and it was such a relief, apart from anything else, after the turmoil of trying to be with Nick.

We had shrugged off the baggage of the previous month and broken the spell by casting a new one. Our theory was that, if the beginning of our romance was so beset with external angst, we could probably handle anything. So it was official. Unofficially official. It just seemed unwise to make it officially official yet; there was a genuine likelihood that Nick might lose it tonight. Part of me resented this – he'd brought this on himself – but I wanted nothing to sully what I had now, and besides, keeping it under wraps was quite fun. As long as I resisted the urge to moon around backstage trilling 'Secret Love' from *Calamity Jane*, everything would be fine. So far so good.

As Betty delivered Concierge's assorted garments and props to the correct dressing rooms – a sci-fi villain outfit for Johnson, Pam Hogg space-goddess cat-suit for Abra, a black and silver Issey Miyake whistle for Nick and a cape covered in tiny LED light-sabers for Kurt (he insisted on wearing his tartan suit as always;

the cape was his compromise) – I took the long trudge up the stone steps to the third floor where Gomez and Carly and his 'chorus' (Gomez's reluctant son Aduki and two over-enthusiastic performing arts students) had been meaningfully banished.

Judging by the grunts, occasional crashes and muffled swearing accompanied by Indian sitar drones and the acrid stench of skunk coming from behind the door of Dressing Room Nine, I guessed that Gomez and co. had already arrived and had embarked on a pre-gig yoga session. I went next door into stuffy, strip-lit Dressing Room Ten, empty except for a few discarded polystyrene cups with lipstick marks on them, and hung up Aviary's costumes on the rail, brushing them down. They didn't look half bad, I mused, listening to the pained yelps, loud exhalations and heavy bumps from next door. I assumed it was yoga they were doing, although one could never be sure with Gomez.

The very idea of any member of Concierge beating the crew to the venue before a show was unlikely, but Gomez had much to prove, not only to his former band-mates, but to the fans. He'd barely admitted it to himself yet, but he was practically preparing to audition for his old band. He missed them, and he'd gone off Carly – the adventure had dried up and was now congealing unpleasantly. Carly was controlling and, intermittently, frightening; Gomez was egotistical and fragile. It was never going to work, but at least, at the very *least*, Gomez assumed that the one positive thing that could come out of this, apart from having the opportunity to dress up as a pretty white bird and really wig out on stage without seeing Nick mouthing "What the *fuck*?" at him, was that he'll have made Concierge miss him. In fact he was sure they already did. He hadn't seen any evidence of this yet but they were proud, he insisted to himself. One night with Kurt and they'd be begging him to come back.

I decided to go back down to the stage. A busy network of people had been beavering away to make my designs come to life, and

I had to admit, they looked impressive even as I peeped from behind the black curtains of the wings. I didn't want them to feel pressured – I trusted them – it was just thrilling to see it all coming together. Sacks of glitter and white feathers were standing by to be cast upon both stage and audience from a height at the correct time, and smoke machines were being tested. There were star-cloths, a craggy, textured floor for Concierge – basically the surface of the moon on acid – separate back-cloths for each act and the flying rig and harness were being set up for Gomez as I watched, a short hairy roadie of a similar size to him being ordered to try them out.

As stressful as it was having myriad extra duties on this tour, I felt grateful to Les. This felt like my new direction. I'd enjoyed the process even if I hadn't realised it until now, and it certainly made a change to ramming malodorous spandex into washing machines or sewing sequins onto jackets. I'd still have to do a bit of that too, but to have been able to sit in a room with Les and the production manager and have my ideas heard rather than shouted over was vindication in itself.

"Well done, man." Les strolled into the wings and slapped me on the back. (Since being granted greater responsibilities, I noticed that Les's treatment of me had become more back-slapping and matey, as if in order to respect my ideas as he would those of a male contemporary, he had to treat me as if I'd actually become male. Hence the fact he'd started calling me 'man' and 'fella'.) "You going to be OK?"

The answer, of course, had to be yes. If I'd said, "Well, actually…" he'd not have been able to accept it, he'd have switched his ears off, walked away. On the other hand, he'd made sure there were no copies of any magazines or newspapers in the venue that made reference to Nick's recent scandal – not just for Nick but for me. He did have a heart. He also didn't want anyone going wobbly on him either. I turned and smiled. "Yes. Thanks. I won't let you down."

"Good. Well, your hard work's done now, so you can kick back for a bit. Have a drink."

"It's 11.30am."

"Well, a coffee or something. Go on. I'll have one if you're making. Milk and two."

Maybe not that much had changed. I headed to the green room and stared at the complicated coffee machine, wiggling the knobs, waiting for it all to make sense before giving it the tried-and-tested whack on the top. It seemed to work: there were a few odd noises and some spluttering and then we were off.

The green room appeared to be a glossy tribute to the decadence this venue had played host to over the past century right up to the studiedly grimy Libertines/Amy Winehouse era. Recent snaps of artists who'd played there were pinned up neatly by the bar like a sneering patchwork quilt; a shiny riot of messy hair, glinting red eyes, lipstick snarls and self-conscious tattoos: middle-class kids trying to get closer to the edge. They made the acts on tonight's bill look like grown-ups, which wasn't normally how I would have described Concierge. It was all relative.

It was strange to think that a band whom, only ten years ago, would have been written off as passé were now fashionable to like again. I'd remembered hearing Vince Neil, the singer from Mötley Crüe, insisting that if you stuck to your guns and didn't bow to trends, you'd come out on top in the end. Judging by how many comebacks were happening in the world of rock and pop, it appeared he was right.

I was proud, it was good to see them getting the attention they deserved, but I also felt a little blue. I loved them but I knew I couldn't stay for much longer; so much had gone down. It was time to move on, and Sam felt the same. Betty had been trying to get me to visualise what I wanted and 'cosmically order' it – she'd read a book by Noel Edmonds and was impressed by how he'd managed to 'manifest' his hit TV series *Deal Or No Deal* with the power of his mind – but the truth was I wasn't sure what I wanted my next step to be. All the same, if Noel could help me conjure something fabulous, preferably something both Sam and I could move on to together, he'd earn my eternal thanks. Hell, I'd even forgive him for Mr Blobby. OK, maybe not.

"Hello."

I was back in the room and Sam was standing in front of me. Sam, in all of his mussed-up magnificence. Maybe there was something in this manifesting malarkey. It might have been daylight outside but in this room it was permanent night; the spotlights were making everything sparkle. He moved towards me and smoothed down the collar on my white shirt-dress.

"Long time no see."

"Three whole hours," I replied. Sam put his arms around my waist only for me to reluctantly shimmy out of his grasp. "Better not. Someone might see us."

"All right. But when… "

"When we're not here. They're a bunch of old gossips. If Nick hears… "

"I don't care about Nick."

"I just don't want anything to spoil it. We've been through enough thanks to him. Besides, I thought you said it was fun keeping it a secret?"

Sam shrugged. "I think it would be more fun to be able to do stuff like hold your hand, tell people you're my girlfriend… " He touched my lips. I opened my mouth and lightly bit his finger.

"Oh my Christ." Betty was in the doorway, quivering at the sight of us. "I knew it," she squeaked, rushing towards us. "I *knew* it was just a matter of time."

"OK, Bet, keep it down!" I laughed, accepting a group hug.

"Yes! Yes, of course." Betty clasped her glittering hands to her chest. "How long?"

"Not long," I said.

"I suppose not, otherwise I'd have picked up the vibes," she said, sitting on the leather sofa and kicking her feet up. "You knew how much I wanted you to get together. You might have mentioned it. I mean, have you… is it proper, like, have you… you know?"

"Betty!"

"Well, there's some stuff I need to do," coughed Sam, slinking out from behind the bar. She was doing it to wind us up, to punish us for being secretive. It was partly that, anyway. But it was partly also because she was utterly shameless.

"It might not be such an issue with Nick," said Betty as I joined her on the couch.

"How so?"

"He's been in therapy three times a week," she said. "That was the agreement because he snuck out of rehab earlier than he should have."

"Oh." The warm lustre that had settled over everything when Sam was in the room, looking at me with his fierce blue eyes, was dissolving.

"He's on methadone now."

"Right." Everybody had been careful not to mention Nick much over the past few weeks, but Betty believed it was time for an update. It felt strange, Nick had already started to fade into never-never territory, and I'd have been happy to let him remain there. That was unrealistic, of course, today of all days.

"And this therapist is working wonders," Betty concluded, picking up my cup and taking a sip.

"He's actually turning up to sessions?"

"Yep,"

"He's not going to… you know… try his luck again now he's getting his confidence back? Do I have to be on my guard?"

Betty paused for a bit too long. "It's early days. You're right to want to keep things a secret when it comes to you and Sam, that's all I'll say."

"And what does that mean, exactly?" I wasn't keen on her uncharacteristically cautious tone. Betty twisted her mouth as she always did when the subject of conversation became delicate.

"It means… well, I think he'd still like to stab Sam with a sharp implement, maybe push him down a big hole. Male ego… and he hasn't really accepted responsibility for… well, anything. But Les is keeping an eye on him. I mean, Nick's got a tour to do. He went to enough trouble busting him out of rehab, he's not going to put up with him going to jail for murder." She let out a cackle and pushed me on the arm when she saw my face. "Joke! GBH at worst."

I attempted a chuckle. As usual, the priorities in Concierge-land were more than a little skewed. "Well, I'm going to keep out of everyone's way tonight, I think," I said. "You can worry about shoulder-pads and moon-boots for a change."

"About time too. I've got a feeling tonight's show will be best enjoyed from out front anyway, and not just because of your set designs, if my trusty cards are not mistaken."

"Oh?"

Betty squealed and clapped her hands. "Wait and see."

Kurt Christmas had arrived, larger than life and louder than anything you could imagine. His tics, which everyone had been asked not to mention, were in full effect and he was exploiting them wildly. He also seemed to find everything absolutely hilarious.

Les was able to breathe a little easier knowing Kurt was in the building, and everyone had been dragged into the green room to greet him. Well, almost everyone.

Sam and I had just handed in our notice to Les, a development he'd been semi-expecting, although he wasn't happy about it. But he generously promised to put a word in for us if he heard of suitable work elsewhere, and decided to keep the news from the band for the time being. We were also allowed to bunk off from Kurt's welcoming committee for obvious reasons. Nick was already in a tricky mood, having pulled out of a pre-arranged interview with *Classic Pop* before the first question had even been asked because he'd decided the journalist looked too much like Sam. Now he was reclining on the couch, feet on the coffee table, face inscrutable as he appraised the monster before him.

"Sir Christmas!" Les was over-compensating for the chill in the air. "Good to see you."

"Likewise, mate!" Kurt shouted. "Haahaha!"

Johnson and Nick looked at each other briefly. They were

both wondering how Kurt could pull this gig off. Could he reach Gomez's high notes? Had he even learnt the songs? It wasn't like anyone would pick him up on it if he hadn't.

"The first thing I want to say is that I'm very happy to be here," said Kurt. "It's an honour to sing with Concierge. I think it will be the beginning of an exciting new chapter for us all." Everyone glanced at Gomez who was maintaining a stoic front.

"Secondly, I'd like to invite you all to a prayer meeting in my dressing room – that's Dressing Room One, naturally – before the show. It really does make a difference to the night ahead. You know, connecting to each other, connecting to God. What do you say, people? 7pm?"

Johnson blinked slowly. "Really?"

"Fuck off!" guffawed Kurt, slapping Johnson hard on the back before twitching madly. It looked as if he was trying to take large bites out of the air. As he recovered from the hilarity of his own joke and the tics subsided, he cast his gaze around the room and settled quickly on the dazzling Abra, who was leaning at the bar. Kurt's eyes shone greedily and everyone tensed up as the inevitable sleaze-fest commenced.

"And how are *you*?" he asked her cleavage as he ambled towards her.

"Erm… " Les stuck out an arm and barred his way.

"Oh sorry, Les. This the wife? Respect, man."

"I'm the bassist, Neanderthal," snarled Abra. Nick smiled faintly, observing the not unfamiliar scene and idly wondering at what point Kurt was going to be punched in the face. Abra simply stalked out of the room.

"No geezers available for the job?" said Kurt. "Although don't get me wrong, it's good to have some tits on stage. Then again, that was always guaranteed at a Concierge show. Eh? Eh? Paha!"

Nick heaved a sigh and slowly recrossed his ankles on the table.

"Shit! It made a sound!" Kurt wheezed.

"She's not a piece of meat, she's a musician like the rest of us," said Nick. "Well, like me, anyway."

"Way to go, sister!" shouted Kurt, fist aloft. "Up the Suffragettes! Wait a minute, I've heard about you – you're the one on smack, right? Explains everything. Check out the strides! Jesus. Don't do drugs, kids."

"Ahahaha!" Les laughed desperately, his hand instinctively reaching his head in a bid to pull out hair that had long since departed. But Kurt had spotted even more irresistible prey. This had just been the warm-up. The real show was about to start.

"Ronald Gomez, as I live and breathe! Been a while. Glastonbury, right?" Kurt lumbered over to Gomez, who was wearing a white lycra unitard and a face like thunder. He was saving the full outfit for the show on strict instructions from Betty and I, much as he wanted to parade around in it.

"Kurt."

"I know we haven't always seen eye to eye, so I've brought you a little offering, an olive branch if you will. LANCE?"

A blond teenager, resplendent in skinny jeans and a low-necked American Apparel tank top, appeared. He was carrying a large object under a satin sheet with ceremonial solemnity. Kurt whacked Lance on the behind and gave him a wink. "Thank you, dear. This is for you, Gomez. I think you'll like it. It's just in case you get a bit peckish before the set."

He whipped off the sheet and revealed a bag of millet. Gomez looked away in disgust and the rest of the band stifled their laughter. Kurt suddenly threw out his left leg like he was kicking an invisible football that had sneaked up on him.

"Oh… " Kurt wiped his face and shook with laughter. "Oh, that was funny."

"Kurt," interjected Les, anxious to prevent any more aggravation. "Maybe we should run the set?" Gomez was apoplectic, barely able to speak.

"Ah, look he's all emotional. Don't mention it, babe," said Kurt. "Anyway, I hear you're going to be laying eggs in your grand finale? Brilliant! Love a good omelette."

"Kurt!" repeated Les hurriedly. He was turning red and had just thrown several antacids into his mouth. "Run a few songs?"

"What? Oh, I suppose so. Let's hope I don't *scramble* my words!" He and Lance broke into laughter as Les tried to guide them towards the stage. "Hey, I'd better not be too good, you guys might try to *poach* me!" He was now bent double, Lance at his side simpering in support. "That would be *oeuf*-shattering, wouldn't it? Ah, poor old Gomez, a shell of the man he was, never could take a yolk." And the puns kept coming as he staggered out. He'd clearly been working on them on the way to the venue. Les looked over his shoulder unhappily at the rest of the band as he went.

"That bastard," hissed Gomez, finally able to speak. "That big, fat… BASTARD."

Abra reappeared, having waited outside until it was a Kurt-free zone.

"Keep it together, Gomez," warned Johnson.

"Yes, rise above it," said Betty. "Channel your anger into energy for the performance."

"You lot weren't much of a support!" Gomez fumed. "Where's your loyalty?"

"Where's yours? You left us, you pranny," said Abra, her Escher-inspired catsuit strobing as she moved. She hadn't even changed for the gig yet, this was just day-wear.

"How dare you?! You didn't even see what he… "

"Christ, will you both shut it?" Everyone gaped at Nick, unaccustomed to him asserting himself through the power of speech. At first they were unsure whether it was actually him, so unfamiliar was the sound of his raised voice. The therapy was working, sort of. "We need to get this fucking sound-check over with. Or is it just going to be me and Kurt?"

Silently everyone filed out, leaving Carly and Gomez simmering by the bar.

"Get Aduki to bring down the costumes. We'll slip them on here after we sound-check," he ordered Carly. "I'd like to watch this."

*

By 8:45pm, Gomez and Carly were back in their dressing room after their Aviary debut. Looking at the two individuals, one could be forgiven for assuming they had both performed at two different gigs. Carly, languishing in her stretchy white unitard, was on a total high. Even though the audience had, with the exception of a handful of die-hard Gomez-heads, laughed and thrown things, as a 'conceptual' performance, everything had gone to plan, from the tricky flying scene right down to the finale. Even so, Gomez was angry. He hadn't moved or spoken for at least ten minutes, but as Carly prepared to sink another tumbler-full of champagne, Gomez leapt up and let out a little scream.

"God, what?" said Carly. "We knew we'd be misunderstood... We don't *want* to be understood."

"It's not about that," snapped Gomez, pacing up and down, glancing at himself occasionally in the mirror. Some of the bulbs around it had broken and the mirror itself was smeared with ancient lipstick. There was no door on the lavatory and as a result the whole room smelt of Toilet Duck and poor aim. This was what you got in Dressing Room Nine. Dressing Room One was a different deal. Kurt Christmas was in Dressing Room One. Kurt was getting the perks, the adulation. He may as well have moved into Gomez's house. Visions of the check-suited behemoth eating Pearl's roast dinners, snorting coke and trading dirty stories with Ange flashed across his mind like a horrible slide-show. Who was to say they hadn't all been getting into the same bed at the end of the night to watch *Desperate Housewives* on DVD, just like they used to with him?

A timid knock at the door pricked the loaded silence.

"WHAT?!" yelled Gomez. Aduki poked his head in. He'd already changed into his black jeans and T-shirt combo and had carefully mussed up his raven-black fringe. Gomez scowled. "Copying Uncle Nick now?" Aduki remained silent. "I know he's been on the telly," Gomez said patronisingly, "and I know he's all dark and mysterious, but trust me, you do *not* want to be like Uncle Nick."

"I'm… erm… just going to watch the show from out front with Kev and Laura now." Aduki scrunched up his face in preparation for the reaction.

"Traitor!" squeaked Gomez. "And who the bloody hell are Kev and Laura when they're at home?"

"They were just on stage with us? The performing arts students?"

"Ponces. Go on, piss off. Enjoy the show. Little prick." He kicked at the door after Aduki had gone.

"What *is* it?" slurred Carly.

"You know what it is."

She banged her empty plastic glass onto the dressing table and yet another bulb made a weak fizzing sound before conking out, the only benefit being that their stuffy little room was now a few degrees cooler. You couldn't open the windows in Dressing Room Nine. They'd been fixed shut after the attempted suicide last year.

"Not this again. Not Kurt Christmas… "

"Yes!" yelled Gomez. "Obviously! I thought he was going to sound bleeding awful in that sound-check but no. He only nailed it. He's only stolen my shitting gig. Even the twitching looked good. I mean, I know he does it a bit on purpose, but— "

"You left," Carly interrupted.

"You made me leave."

"I didn't have to try very hard."

"You fucking kidnapped me!"

"I thought it would make them appreciate you more."

"You had your own twisted reasons for what you did," said

Gomez. "Anyway, why are we suddenly talking about you? This is about me! Me! Me! The point is they now seem to appreciate Kurt more. So thanks for that, Carly. Thank you very much."

"But Gomez, what about… "

"Don't say it. Don't even think about it. If you think I want to traipse around doing Aviary for the rest of my working life, you've got another thing coming. I belong with *that* band down *there*." He jabbed a finger towards the staircase. "The band that is about to go on and perform an exclusive warm-up gig for a whopping great space-age-themed tour. That's what I'm supposed to be doing."

He grabbed the keys and charged out of the dressing room. Carly sprang up to stop him but he slammed the door and locked it behind him, leaving her screeching drunkenly and thumping the door with her fists.

I settled into my seat at the front of the balcony next to Ange and Pearl. Sam and the other technicians had left the stage after a final check of the instruments and the hazardous set; Les was chewing his nails in the wings with the rest of the band. The lights dimmed, the audience started to roar, many of them defiantly chanting Gomez's name, and the walk-on music began. Les had chosen the opening theme to the movie *Moon* by Clint Mansell. It was contemporary but suitably dramatic, and Concierge loved a bit of drama. This was just as well because at that very moment, Gomez was running towards the stage to create a drama of considerable size.

Little did he know this was exactly what Les wanted, what he expected. He knew Gomez's ego would never withstand the flack that Aviary attracted, even less could it withstand seeing Kurt making a successful debut as the new frontman of Concierge. It was all going to plan.

26

"And what do you think you're doing?" said Les, physically stopping Gomez in his tracks as he strutted towards the stage. The show had already begun – so much the better. This would suit his grand entrance perfectly.

"I am getting *my* gig back!" Gomez shouted, barely audible over the monstrous sound of Concierge's opening number. The response from the crowd was mixed to say the least. Kurt sounded terrible, a far cry from his impressive performance in the sound-check. It was as if he was deliberately singing off key. Gomez struggled in vain against Les's strength. "Get off me, you lummox! That should be me out there."

Les smiled and shook his head. "Just listen to that. That's one happy audience. Mostly."

"Bollocks! I can hear booing." He wriggled as Les gripped him firmly by the arms.

"Let it go, Gomez." Les released him and then peered around the corner of the wings at the press pit. There were plenty of photographers, snapping furiously. Soon Kurt would bring out the big guns. What would follow would ultimately do everyone plenty of favours.

"Ladies and gentlemen," boomed Kurt. "It gives me great pride to stand before you tonight as the new singer of Concierge!"

He'd been expressly instructed to annunciate these last five words. The booing increased in ferocity. Someone threw a bobble hat on stage. Les smiled as Gomez turned white at his side, the wings of his costume shaking.

"It's time for a fresh start," continued Kurt. "But please raise your drinks to the fine work of my predecessor... erm... shit. I can't remember his name." And with that he threw his head back and laughed. A plastic pint glass flew towards him.

A roar went up in the crowd, and that roar was for Gomez, who was rushing as fast as his prohibitively tight costume could allow towards Kurt. He took a running leap and clamped himself onto his target, thumping him as the fans screamed their approval and the cameras flashed.

Kurt had promised Les he wouldn't fight back, wouldn't even laugh at him. It was important that the fans could respect him, which was already proving a challenge considering that, from the audience's point of view, there he was, dressed in a winged unitard which left little to the imagination, attempting to beat up a large man in a sparkly cape. However, if the baying and chanting was anything to go by, everyone in the crowd was now more on Gomez's side than ever.

After a few more seconds of pummelling, Gomez staggered backwards, spent. He looked up at Johnson who eyed him severely from behind the drums – he still hadn't quite forgiven him.

"Gomez," said Kurt woodenly into the microphone, reading the words Les had asked him to say. "This is madness. You are the true frontman of Concierge. I'm going to do the right thing. I'm stepping down." And with that, he ceremoniously took off his twinkling cape and placed it around Gomez's shoulders before handing over his guitar. The fans were loving it. Les caught Kurt's eye from the wings and nodded his approval for the performance. He wasn't going to win any Oscars but Les didn't care, Kurt had completed the job he'd been paid to do. The crowd went wild. Gomez was back.

Les took out the cigar he'd secreted upon his person in readiness for this moment and sauntered out into the street. He half-listened to the opening chords of their 1985 classic 'Late Check Out' as he looked up at the moon. The stage door banged. Les looked round to see Kurt ambling towards him, cape-free and beaming, sweat patches darkening his ubiquitous suit.

"How was that?"

"Excellent," said Les, taking a wodge of cash from his inside pocket and handing it over. "Normal service has been resumed, thanks to you. And me, obviously. It was my idea."

"Naturally. It's sad, really," said Kurt, pocketing the cash. "I could have got used to being in Concierge. Pity they all hate me."

"If you want to make an omelette, without wishing to steal one of your earlier puns, you have to break some eggs," insisted Les, patting Kurt on the shoulder. "And if you'd been nicer the others might have wanted you to stick around. They're not mad about Gomez either, you know. I just needed that band back together." Les chomped on his cigar and continued gazing at the moon as the theatre throbbed behind them. He secretly assumed that not all of Kurt's bluster was an act, but it was fair to say it had been ramped up for Concierge's benefit.

Kurt nodded and pulled on a joint that had been pre-rolled by Lance earlier that evening. Les was happy. Mission Gomez was accomplished. He just had one more good deed he wanted to do.

"What are the Idiots doing right now?"

"Well, it sounds to me like they're just about to wrap up that awful song about checking out, if I'm not mistaken," dead-panned Kurt. "Oh wait, you mean my band."

"Don't push it."

"Big tour coming up," he said, a haze of smoke hanging in front of his face like a screen. "We set off late November, big Christmas gig at the Forum and then off to the States for three months. Should keep us in beer and fags for a bit."

"Right. If I had my way, I'd hang onto these two myself but

this is the kind of caring, sharing man I am. Two of my favourite crew-members have resigned. Personal reasons. They're going to work out a bit of notice and then that's it. I don't think they've got any plans beyond that yet. Is there any chance the Idiots need a designer and a tech? You'll have met Sam already, nice bloke."

"Northern? Blond? Seems a personable cove."

"And Sylvie is… "

"The one who went out with Dracula. I know the one. Mary Pickford after a bender." He gave a manic snort that reminded Les of Rik Mayall in *The Young Ones*. "I'll take 'em," said Kurt, as if he was buying a pair of shoes.

Les was prepared to do a bit more selling but if this was all it took… "Well, they don't know I'm talking to you about this, I just wanted to put a word in as I can recommend them, and as they're in the market for— "

"I said, I'll take 'em," repeated Kurt, sounding increasingly stoned. "We can use them. Besides," he added, leaning into Les with an evil glint, "it'll be good to have a bit of crumpet in the entourage."

"Now Kurt," said Les. "Not this again. Sylvie has been through enough without— "

"Cool your boots, I'm joking." He wasn't. "Anyway, who says I was talking about Sylvie? Eh?" He winked at Les and took another drag before strolling back inside, chuckling to himself and rubbing his hands together.

"Basically, you have the choice of travelling on the Booze Bus or the Speed Bus," explained Gordo, the perpetually weary tour manager of the Idiots. Sam and I looked up at the tour buses, shining, dark, clean (so far). "Plenty of room on both," Gordo yawned. "The Booze Bus is presided over by three of the Idiots: Colin, who plays bass, Wolfie, slide guitar, and Brian. He's on vibe control and dancing, percussion, that kind of thing. Yes, a bit like Bez," he added, before either of us could suggest it. He'd done this before. "And," concluded Gordo. "The Speed Bus transports Kurt, whom you know, Boggle the drummer and Psycho Geoff."

"Booze Bus, please," we said simultaneously, relieved to have a choice. We hauled our cases towards the bus that already contained Wolfie and Colin, who'd arrived early and appeared to be working their way through the broadsheets.

"Good choice," said Gordo. "See you on there in a bit."

As I approached the doors, I observed that Wolfie was, as one might expect, dark and hairy, but more noticeably he was also wearing a pair of pince-nez and a deer-stalker, and was sedately flicking through *The Financial Times*. Colin, seated opposite, wore a three-piece suit and was sipping what was probably a very expensive single malt. It was 10am.

Sam and I had to admit, since agreeing to work with the Idiots, our income had shot up, our stress levels had dropped and the anxiety we'd felt latterly around Concierge had faded into memory – as long as we kept out of Kurt's way when he was feeling horny, we'd be fine.

Wolfie and Colin looked up as the newbies got on board.

"Hullo," grunted Wolfie.

"Welcome aboard," said Colin, taking another sip of whisky before getting up to pour two more glasses from a beautiful built-in drinks cabinet. It was like something out of a P.G. Wodehouse novel.

"Thanks," I murmured, looking around in wonder. "I have to say, I wasn't expecting this. It's so— "

"Civilised?" said Wolfie. "We like it like this. We prefer to save our energy for the show nowadays." And with that they returned to their newspapers. We quietly moved to the back seat, reluctant to disturb these gentlemen any further. We couldn't imagine Colin or Wolfie being in a band like the Idiots. We hadn't even met Brian yet, but he was probably cut from a similar tweedy cloth. Maybe they were madder than Kurt once they got onstage. But then that was the business: theatre, illusion, smoke and mirrors, at least for those who intended to stay the course in one piece. I looked out of the window to see the moon, like an old friend, rising in the clear afternoon sky, lacy and pale as a ghost, growing in strength and size.

"Well… " said Sam. "How nice."

"Indeed."

Wolfie, sensing we were feeling inhibited, got up and walked to the stereo, putting on a Chet Baker CD to give Sam and I a barrier to talk behind. After perusing the back of the album cover, he sat back down and flapped open his newspaper again.

"We could always go on the Speed Bus just the once," said Sam as the bus slowly started to move. "You know, at some point on the tour. To see what it's like."

"Definitely. Just the once, as you say." For now, I was happy to curl up on the soft, leather seat and enjoy the peace. It wouldn't last.

Sam was falling into a doze, lulled by the purr of the bus as it made its stately way through West London. I gently took the iPod from his jeans pocket and scrolled through the albums down to 'M'. There it was. I closed my eyes as the city flashed past, and grey turned to green.

FURTHER LISTENING – HIGHLIGHTS FROM THE CONCIERGE TOUR BUS PLAYLIST:

Gomez:
'It Doesn't Have To Be This Way' – The Blow Monkeys
'Union Of The Snake' – Duran Duran
'Licence To Kill' – Gladys Knight
'Princes Of The Universe' – Queen
'Hot Stuff' – Donna Summer
'Small Talk' – Scritti Politti

Nick:
'Transmission' – Joy Division
'Spell' – Nick Cave and The Bad Seeds
'Violaine' – The Cocteau Twins
'Nineteen Hundred And Eighty Five' – Wings
'Need You Tonite' – Mylo
'Elevation' – Television

Johnson:
'I Want More' – Can
'Fade To Grey' – Visage
'Being Boiled' – The Human League
'Hounds Of Love' – Kate Bush
'Peg' – Steely Dan
'Station To Station' – David Bowie

Abra:
'Baby, I'm A Star' – Prince
'Upside Down' – Diana Ross
'Debaser' – The Pixies
'Fall In Love With Me' – Iggy Pop
'Little Miss Lover' – Jimi Hendrix
'Hit It And Quit It' – Funkadelic

Les:

'You Send Me' – Aretha Franklin
'Girl, You'll Be A Woman Soon' – Neil Diamond
'American Woman' – The Guess Who
'Misty Mountain Hop' – Led Zeppelin
'Brother Doctor, Sister Nurse' – Mickey Jupp
'Gone Hollywood' – Supertramp

ACKNOWLEDGMENTS

Eternal thanks to my incredibly supportive husband Dylan Howe who has helped immeasurably in the shaping of this book. Thanks and love to my family, Janey Preger (for *I'm Dead – How Are You?*), Marzipan the cat for keeping me company during long nights of writing, everyone on Facebook who came up with hilarious suggestions for character names and possible book titles – they crack me up every time I think of them. Louise Rhind-Tutt, Jane Bradley, Mark Ellen, Kirsty Allison, Phill Jupitus, Gideon Coe. Everyone at Matador, particularly my editorial coordinators Becky Millar and Lauren Lewis, marketing whizz Jasmin Elliott and production controllers Jack Wedgbury, Rosie Lowe, production manager Jennifer Parker, and everyone who took the time to enthuse, encourage, advise and inspire, directly or indirectly. And you, for picking up this book. I hope you enjoy it.